The Watch On The Beach
Emily B. Scialom

Acknowledgements

Thank you infinitely to my dear friend and ally, William Hartston, for the invaluable insights and editorial advice. As has always been the case, I am sure that this literary offering wouldn't be half as good without your involvement.

I would also like to give my most heartfelt gratitude to Tony Blackmur for the exquisite cover design. Your assistance through the years has meant so much.

Author Biography

Emily Bollington Scialom was born in Hackney, London on July 27th 1984. She was raised in Glastonbury before relocating to Cambridge with her family in 1996.

She became a nationally published poet aged eight and an internationally published poet at the age of seventeen before her debut novel, 'The Religion Of Self-Enlightenment', was published by Olympia in 2016. A second novel, 'The Rivers' (Austin Macauley), followed in 2019.

'Eternal Artist'(2020), 'My Searches For Meaning' (2021) and 'Viajes Internos' (2022) were three poetic offerings released in quick succession prior to the publication of her third novel, 'A Moment Of Perfection' in 2022.

'The Watch On The Beach' is, therefore, her seventh release in seven years.

In loving memory of Rufus Fox, who is surely now wreaking havoc amidst the angels.

Prologue

I awoke sloppy, insolent towards hospital staff and concerned helpers alike. Life was no longer what I wanted and I remained in this world wholly against my wishes. Truthfully, I was afraid. Not of dying, my drawing closer to a potentially elevated plain of existence, but of the agony that would come through continuing to live. This world was not for me and I couldn't understand how anyone could feel joy, even artificially, in such a realm.

The ward felt cold, but not as icy as my interpretations of the divine: my beloved deity, I believed, had seen me struggling to break my mortal chains, but had not the grace to grant me release. What a God! What a world! What a sorry state of being I seemingly had no choice but to surrender to.

"Clara? Can you hear me?"

Unfortunately, I could - I nodded to confirm this fact.

"You're safe now," the nurse assured her in a syrupy voice which in my view belied the cruelty of the world the medical professional was a part of. As a homeless person screaming for help with no response offered from a crowded street, my desperation to escape my body had been unanimously ignored – even prohibited.

Still, even if the nurse was paid to do so at least someone feigned care for me. Recovery seemed the only option, though I was loath to choose it.

However, before building a future I had to first survey the past.

Every day after I regained consciousness felt uphill at a variety of angles, though I was unable to comfortably navigate any of them. I also found in the midst of the process of rebuilding my life that so many former allies turned around and laughed at my misfortune from lofty heights of contentment and holistic wellbeing, emotional states I had tragically not experienced for some time: unlike physical distress, mental imbalance did not tend to evoke sympathy.

There had been many who had seen me drowning throughout my descent and did not reach out for fear of going down with this ship. The storms which abounded did not threaten their own vessels and they were happiest to distance themselves as my tragedy unfolded.

Some had even claimed that they could not see me at all, did not even know me; the memories of our happier times together were smothered into insignificance. While resigned to the muraled walls of Addenbrooke's all of the moments my tortured mind deemed worthy of recollection seemed either warped misinterpretations or cruel expositions of my current nadir.

How far I had come from my carefree childhood days spent running through fields in full bloom, yet how far I was from the wisdom of old age and hindsight. I resigned myself to the no man's land betwixt the two, knives of discontentment sharpening with every passing second.

Still, in my extensive questing I had not been left empty-handed: I had learnt that one must find purpose even when there appears to be none, each of us must find a spark of fire to potentially warm the immeasurable darkness which at times engulfs us all. It is a measure of our ability to survive that we are able to source self-love in a world seeped in violence and hatred. However, I must confess I did not relish the task.

At first every day tasted more sour than the last and each moment brought new aspects of reality to fear. The blood which had poured from my wrists had traumatised my conscious mind as much as the thought of my untold tomorrows.

It was little wonder, I thought to myself in a moment of rare clarity, that many hid from their pain in caves of delusion for most of their pitiful lives. After all, who wants to dwell on our finite nature and the counterfeit sense of joy to the dreams which kept us alive?

A few weeks passed - eventually numbness overwhelmed me and I simply forgot to be afraid or unhappy, submerged as I was by the pressing need to endure. However, the physical scars would not entirely heal just as the dull ache in my soul had never totally ceased, much as I willed it to and took precautions against its more threatening elements.

As with most things my attempts to be entirely healthy were essentially futile and the deep, raw shame at who I had become caused every mundane moment to overflow with disappointment. Yet somehow I careered onwards, tied to a pulse and its accompaniments as a weak prisoner desperate for emancipation.

Looking back at my previous lifestyle (which now seemed so far behind me), I guess drugs had seemed the easiest available means of escape from uncomfortable feelings. I had soon practised my newfound religion with devotion. I had prayed everyday with rings of smoke for words. I had fallen to my knees in both awe and relief as multi-faceted emotions replaced a dull grey brick wall of despair, I cowered in abject fear as my demons mutated and multiplied; all of my brave attempts at sincere inner work eventually came to be accompanied by chemicals. The ancient and modern intermingled in terms of both the substances in my bloodstream and the language that flowed from my pen; shakily scrawled truth tells its own story.

Perhaps I had foolishly obeyed Rimbaud when he had called for the disorientation of the senses more than God when He called for righteousness from His children. After all, everyone believed in something: the vacuum of my faith in time had become filled by literature.

I had always written because I had to, not for an abstract sense of leisure. Without words I felt totally alone, yet with self-expression often came understanding.

In being given a reprieve from death, or at least a stay of execution, I found I had the time and desperate need to reassess my journey to these new horizons of sorrow. I picked apart and analysed memories as shards of a shattered life: the descent into my emotional abyss had been far steeper than I had expected, though I had indeed managed to distinguish from my tornado of emotions the sensation of free falling from the very start.

After I left Addenbrooke's and returned to my childhood home, weeks turned into months of agonising retribution and self-analysis. I found that some of my recollections were disturbing, alarming or rendered blurry by overwhelming trauma. My constant lack of ability to recall names seemed a symptom of a disease that would eventually see me forget and disregard my very self.

For good reason did I sense myself to be one of God's more rushed creations: as I pickpocketed the past for any shrapnel of understanding, I found myself having ever decreasing amounts of respect for who I was and what I stood for. Yet all was not lost and I came to see an opportunity to correct my numerous mistakes in the future: I could start afresh, change direction on my pathway and find my dharma, my tribe, my purpose.

As I lay capsized in my single bed, paralysed by overwhelming sensations and thoughts, I would close my eyes every time a memory rolled over me as a wave and found myself to be merely a surfer of the tides. Almost from the moment I opened my eyes in the hospital I began to formulate my version of events and as time relentlessly continued to pass I sensed an increasingly pressing need to externalise my innermost turmoil.

The result was to become my debut novel, a book of questionable appeal that was as disjointed and convoluted as my recollections had inevitably come to be. It was important mainly to me in my quest for sanity, but that did not render it worthless.

As I wrote I became increasingly horrified at the monster I had previously been, yet the question of how to apportion blame between myself and the wider world troubled me for I knew I wasn't alone in my struggle to remain here: I had often encountered - perhaps at certain points even been surrounded by – those who were visibly struggling to cope.

Such collective suffering could not merely be the fault of individuals, but must instead be a more widespread and systemic issue. In my experience loneliness was as universal as despair; such vivid and uncomfortable feelings were connected as an umbilical cord to a womb: that, quite simply, was life.

I was determined not to hate life forever, though, and as the healing process progressed I yearned to feel rays of love for myself and my humble existence stream from my whole heart. It may have been a distant dream, requiring years to fulfil, yet every sentence I diligently scrawled was a step in the right direction, a small victory to be celebrated.

A year later, in 2018, my story was complete and I felt I had something to show for my troubles. I did not anticipate an ecstatic audience and self-published to little fanfare, but that scarcely mattered in my eyes: my cry had become audible, my opinions vaguely formulated and my heart now had a window of words.

Chapter One

I was lost, though I knew it not: it was the summer of my youth, but I had already been navigating the complex mazes of dangerous relationships and the uncomfortable emotions they evoke for too many years. In all my interactions with others, however, I remained unchallenged in my habit of looking down on the most prestigious of my fellow Cambridge dwellers with their tin cup accolades and corrupt acquisition of academic achievements. After all, judgemental attitudes were rife wherever I looked. To me at the time at least, such feats laid bare the ridiculous human need for objectively meaningless competition between the numerous divided parts of a singular whole.

Meanwhile I had been all too aware that my casual condescension was so much more passionately mirrored by the victims of it, for I was declared to be almost entirely without conventional merit.

"You're a credit to your parents" was not a compliment I heard often in general and it was also praise I was never likely to receive: I was a product of my parents, but not a credit to them.

I lived on the outskirts of the city with my long-suffering mother, Louise, in a simple, two-bedroom house on a neglected council estate. Louise had married into the Cook family, yet when my father eventually divorced her and made his opinions about fatherhood perfectly clear as his only child I legally obtained my Mum's maiden name. Thus the

Reynolds' household in its eventual, overly long incarnation was born.

It had a small garden where I would smoke and think whenever the urge to do so came to me. Though I was chained to flesh and bone, I was vaguely free to contemplate the perils and blessings of such a position as well as life beyond my own fragile mortal shell.

I could not escape the glaring nature of my imperfection, though others very kindly informed me that I was relatively pleasing to the eye with my long hair and sensual curves. I was primarily unsure how to receive such compliments, but I would also question whether to be thankful or resentful about this: after all, any hint of aesthetic beauty inevitably attracted predators.

From a young age us girls were taught to beautify ourselves endlessly, forever to be discontent with our bodies and appearances. However, in doing so I felt we were simply making ourselves ever more vulnerable to unwanted sexual advances and even assaults from those who were never taught better. It seemed to me as though, despite some progress in the quest for equal rights, the patriarchy was still so embedded into global culture that women and girls were sinisterly encouraged to dig their graves, being worthless in the eyes of the ignorant.

Nevertheless, I was brave, even brash, in my interactions with the opposite sex. I had many lovers; I also endured my fair share of lonely nights. Among my acquaintances I also had a multitude of partners in crime, but I was ultimately painfully alone. I pretended to be relatively politically informed, yet simple questions uncovered the vast extents of my ignorance. I tended to pride myself solely on self-neglect.

While reflecting upon my younger years I found that shyness was a constant theme and yet it seemed to me that such a quality was indicative of an inflated sense of self-importance. When I blushed at the whirling of my inner world, what did my audience care for my inner torture?

No, I would tell myself that shyness was for those who took life and themselves far too seriously. Still I could not help my nature and found myself caring ever more deeply about most things in spite of a desire for the comforts of apathy. The only thing I didn't care for was metal music: I found its anger and chaos infectious rather than cathartic as some suggested it to be.

The intense emotional conflicts which plagued the foreground of my mind occasionally retreated and at such points I felt relatively privileged to have lived a portion of my youth free from the global horrors which now swamped the mainstream news. It seemed, as the environmental crisis rapidly developed, that kids were now having their futures snatched away from them, the world seemingly ending before the lives of the young had truly begun.

Of course, I naturally had my worries - as all did. My Mum constantly berated me for the state of my general existence: the lack of financial security, romantic nourishment or secure friendships rendered my presence more of a burden than an asset.

I found myself to be in a bizarre world full of injustice and inequality. Where was the empathy and compassion to be found? I concluded in my pondering that one must mine such qualities within as though precious minerals in order to survive. However, evidently few were digging.

The outsiders I mingled with may have been well read, but their existential conclusions were often illegitimate and nuanced; as was the case with myself, these were the kinds of people who were not defined or confined by traditional perceptions of life.

My problems began to mount during the turbulent year of 2016. At the beginning of the year, on January 5th, I had turned 28 years old. As the years passed I had grown to embrace my physical features after spending my developmental years drowning in self-loathing. My curly dark hair, dark eyes and fair skin became familiar enough to accept eventually; any perceived differences from others were even celebrated in time due to my drifting from an insider to an outsider in terms of social circles. My most remarked upon physical feature was my skin colour: I was so pale that some suspected make-up and cruelly said I looked like a ghost. As I say, in due course I paid no mind, though when I first heard such comments they cut like knives.

During the evenings of that time I would retreat from the mocking crowds, in turns muttering to myself and smoking under the moon and stars overlooking my Mum's house in a worryingly standard exhibition of my borderline insanity.

"But do the greatest geniuses have the worst mental afflictions? Is the extent of the madness proportional to the measure of ingenuity?"

One more cigarette underneath the moonlight and I decided that I really had to stop these abstract musings. Still, I could not help but indulge myself.

"Does the craziness inform the art? Can you have a day without a night?" I had an uncomfortable habit of continuing down such mental worm holes almost involuntarily.

"Some people have no ambition and achieve nothing. Others have minimal ambition and find modest success. Some with average ambitions either reach their goals or don't. Some at every level exceed their tame and mediocre dreams, but..."

I dragged hard on my nicotine supply.

"...those with grand ambitions often fail. A very few who have bombastic visions fulfil them. Fewer still exceed all previously conceived of ambitions, flying directly into the sun of history."

I inhaled the last of my plentiful toxins and made my conclusion: "These are the dreamers, those who carve the future using their bare imaginations and the majesty of Karmic Law, which governs all things."

My belief in karma alienated me from Western culture (of which I was only a fringe part) because the West showed no awareness of such a concept: people all around me were treated as fossil fuels to be burned up or annihilated for profit.

I often pondered whether or not I had been born in the wrong time, in the wrong place or to the wrong people. Were such things possible? Perhaps I belonged in rural India during the time of the Buddha.

A cosmic misunderstanding had taken place, I was sure of it, but in reorganising my mental whirlwind I let these ideas and feelings quietly slip quietly into the background to reside with my many other subconscious confusions. I didn't want to make a fuss.

Despite being regularly named one of the very finest places to live in England, as well as sporadically claiming global attention for the advances made in academia, arts and science within its borders, Cambridge remained a sleepy realm in the eyes of many of the locals. So much so that it was labelled "Samebridge" by the witty and overly expectant inhabitants who called it home. These folks were generally waiting for an event to spark excitement, or even condemnation, but there was precious little fuel for their emotional fire: mostly things did, indeed, remain vaguely monotonous.

The city was famous predominantly for its university; most of the permanent residents were paid as little attention as possible. In response an alternative anarchic subculture had formed almost as an enemy of conventional academic teachings. This was the strata of society which I came to call home.

Unlike the big northern cities or the metropolis of central London, Cambridge felt a bit out of the way. Yes, there was a constant bustle of tourists and students, but even those felt somehow monochrome.

The hallowed halls of Cambridge University and the spiralling towers of the churches in the centre of the city, though striking to behold, meant fairly little to me as I usually wished to be somewhere else: I found the snobbery and coldness of the people of Cambridge tiring at best and repulsive at worst, a symptom of the wider historical struggles involving class, race and gender. In a world of haves and have nots nowhere was the gap between the two so acute as within this scenic city of no more than 140,000 residents.

One sleepy Tuesday in late January, the precise day having been confirmed upon waking after some confusion, I crawled out of bed to venture into the city centre. I eventually made my way up the creaky stairs to my dealer's top floor apartment in order to obtain my usual substances. Yet in casually investigating the room I soon noticed something curious in a drawer. After enquiring I was told "That's just codeine. You can get it on prescription, but you only need it if you're in pain."

The last of his simple words struck a chord in me so loud and clear that I almost looked up at the ceiling to give thanks to God. I sure did believe in God, but couldn't for the eternal life of me follow His or Her or Its madcap rules: creating a world full of drugs and then banning people from using them seemed a bizarre aspect to a supposed masterplan.

Given my current mental frailty and spiritual dissonance I ordered as much codeine as I could possibly afford: it must be the drug I had been looking for all my life, I thought as I closed the door with a smile.

The darkness was closing in and the hours elongated. On my way home I bumped into a casual acquaintance. Lazy Jim or Sneaky or whatever he was actually called - I was so bad with names. It's actually recognised as a genuine medical condition which, ironically, has a name which I could seemingly never properly recall.

Lazy Tim (or whatever) was the kind of shady individual who would snort all the available drugs and then expect his company to play counsellor, exploring the full details of his heritage with no omissions or short tracks. In other words his cheek was the only aspect of the solar system which could compare in scale to Jupiter.

"Sorry, can't stop," I said bustling past as he tried his best to harass me, the wind biting at my neck as though I was prey.

"Sweetheart, do you know what the most geologically active object in the solar system is?"

As an opening question this pretty much floored me. I confessed to my shame that I did not.

"Io, the innermost moon of Jupiter. It has around 300 active volcanoes and looks like a tie-dyed marble."

Now that was really something. At last someone

had truly spoken to me. I decided to prolong my bitterly cold journey home and get a pint with what's-his-face instead. I had no blow left anyway, so the danger of an overwrought session seemed minimal.

I walked into the nearest pub to the familiar senses of judgement and rejection intermingling. The same faces sipped their beers in the same despair they had been in for years. What could I possibly do to help them?

"I'll have a strawberry and lime cider, please."

A cider was fetched.

"What can I get you?" The question, directed at my companion, was hard to hear over the mostly nonsensical mutterings occurring around me. But Sneaky Tom recognised the gist of the interaction well, pointed and received.

"So how've you been?" I ignited a conversation I was unsure I wanted to be a part of in the first place, but sensing myself to be part-way through a maze I could only venture onwards.

"My wife left me, darling. That's why I've been doing so much space research: I need something to take my mind off things."

I brushed aside the cut-and-paste pity and the ill-advised conversation was prematurely dealt a fatal injury.

"It was probably for the best," was my blunt conclusion, given without the required evidence or sympathy. There are few things less palatable than the truth and drinks were consumed rapidly from that point on.

"Excuse me? What would you know of marriage and the sacrifices that lifelong commitments entail?"

"Perhaps I see the cliff at the end of the pathway and refuse the journey. Anyway, as that Incubus song says: 'Temporary-ism has been the black plague and the Jesus of our age.' Most things are temporary these days; perhaps it was time to move on."

"Perhaps you have a heart of stone!"

My acquaintance was losing patience with me, but on account of my gender he was reluctant to choose violence in public.

Besides this theory of my heartlessness, I had to admit, had the ring of truth. Every time I practised self-analysis it resulted in my feeling undeserving of a pulse and all that it brings. I was in no mood for an argument, though: I made my excuses and left.

It started to rain, so I took shelter under the big, broad trees on Jesus Green. Keen to be rid of my pressing sense of abstract agony, I gobbled some of the good stuff while praying for these inner and outer downpours to subside.

Chapter Two

Memories of what had become the night before became clearer now that I had properly slept and I was at last able to ponder them. I had marched from Jesus Green to the other side of town and paid a visit to my mate Carl, promptly snorted some K and passed out.

Upon waking I found myself eavesdropping on a most convoluted dialogue. Although they had similar ages, weights and appearances that was as far as Carl and his visitor, Jimmy, would eventually find their connections went. Still, even their initially stuttered communicative embarkation did not suggest the fracas that was to follow. They were both far too gone for words, anyway: their conversational positions were untenable from the point of introduction.

"127 and 271 are very different numbers, though they may look similar. In the same way two people may look the same, but have very different senses of self-worth (maybe even objective worth). Yet without every number in existence there could only be 0 and with every number you make infinity," Jimmy clumsily declared.

"What are you on about?" Carlos replied bluntly.

"I'm saying although we are all made up of the same materials the results vary wildly."

"It's just a simple anagram, obviously. What are you looking for? Approval? Someone to applaud your every utterance?"

Jimmy tried to explain.

Carl wouldn't let him waste his breath. "No! You're looking for a revelation. Prowling and digging here and there until you find it."

Jimmy looked at him as a deer in headlights.

"Well, I want to know the answers. All of them. I mean, what should I realise before I die?"

Carl looked Jimmy dead in the eyes.

"Listen, you say you want to really know life, but the truth is most people don't want revelations. They want to live a life they despise for 80 years and then wake up screaming, knowing they've wasted it all. Most are programmed to be a part of a system that's destroying the planet, living out these narratives to the bitter end. Epistemophobia is more common than the word suggests."

"Oh, here we go! Throwing around long words now, are we? What's that mean, clever clogs?"

"It means fear of knowledge, you doughnut. It's worse than ignorance - it's wilful ignorance!"

"Huh. I'd never thought about it like that before..."

"Revelations make people uncomfortable, take them too close to the edge. I prefer to think of the world through the lens of physics. For example, have you ever sat and meditated on how miraculous it is that every atom in the universe stays in place, completely dependent on all of the others?"

"I don't dig science much," Jimmy declared shamelessly.

As I stirred on the bed in the corner of the room, I could see that Carl was taken aback by this.

"What kind of idiocy are you speaking now? Who doesn't dig science - it's the study of what is?"

Jimmy stood firm. "No, I don't buy it. Maybe in its purest form this is the case, but these days science is too bloated, arrogant and greedy: science leaves no magic for the rest of us."

Carl was incensed by what he perceived to be his company's profound ignorance.

"Have you ever read 'The Magic Of Reality' by Dawkins? No, I didn't think so. It's all about how the universe is so magical that we don't need anything more. No belief in fairies or goblins..."

He trailed off, believing he had made his point adequately and distracted by the important task of rolling another joint.

"I guess I've always wanted revelations. And maybe to see a fairy, too! It is perhaps these things which make me different," Jimmy said, perceiving himself to be clever.

"Is that your big revelation then? That you're different? Dude, we're all different around here!"

Carl gestured broadly to either side of his person, encouraging Jimmy to shift his attention to the train going by outside, a means of escape. Jimmy then wished he was either on the train or under it, close as he was to the suicidal feelings he had when he was a teenager: as a giant circle, his emotions seemed to revolve through the years.

All the while he wondered: "What's so wrong with wanting revelations? Surely that's the opposite of epistemography or whatever?"

But Jimmy failed to change his most real

thoughts into words in the brief hours he spent with Carlos and my groggy, semi-conscious self. The two men soon changed subjects to those of a more mundane nature. Aliens, God and the unknown lurked in the shadows of their minds; conversational subjects as unwanted as ex-friends.

Disjointed, intoxicated and somewhat nonsensical conversations such as these were taking place all across the city, if not the world.

Towards the end of the session Carl was quiet for a long time as if thinking of something remarkable. He excavated his mind and emerged with what he believed to be verbal treasure: "It's the same with 'sacred' and 'scared'."

It was now Jimmy's turn to be lost in a fog of confusion.

"What?"

Carl continued. "You know, what you were trying to say earlier about numbers being the same but different. It works with words too, you see? 'Dog' and 'God' is another one. I don't much enjoy maths, seems to me as though it's another bloody religion. Numbers aren't my deities."

"What IS your deity, Carly boy?" Jimmy said with a cheeky smile.

"Freedom," Carl replied, dead serious. "If anything gets in the way of my freedom it has to go. Numbers can chain people: earnings, bills, ages. The key is to discard numbers, escape them. And Lord knows there's no greater escape than words. Words ARE freedom. It's even in The Bible - words are the origin, man. If you can communicate as you wish there are no barriers between your inner and outer worlds. Too many people live in more or less agonising states of repression."

"I don't believe in words just like you don't believe in things you can't see. Watch this..."

Jimmy ventured over to the window, opened it as wide as possible and screamed with unrestrained venom at the nearest passing stranger: "I HOPE YOU DIE OF AIDS!" These were the words he chose, out of all the options presented by the English language, to communicate to his fellow human.

"Now THAT'S freedom," Jimmy said with a perverse, beaming face.

I was shocked into complete consciousness by the volume and toxicity of Jimmy's outburst, though I was unsure how to intervene.

"No, that's hate speech, you cunt!" Carl retorted, apologising to the innocent passing man and closing the curtains. The stranger was now looking in their direction, but had seemingly not even heard (or else could not believe what he had heard). Carl had witnessed quite enough, though, and Jimmy was roughly escorted from the premises.

Having stirred fully awake in the commotion, my first contribution to proceedings was to shout "nominal aphasia!" as if I'd found the meaning of it all.

Chapter Three

I had decided that I needed a change of scenery
after such a distressing scene at Carl's. An hour
south of Cambridge in the heart of London, two
men and a woman were talking when I emerged on
the scene with jovial greetings, fresh from the train
station with wet hair and optimistic expectations of
a good time.

We sat together in a pub in Camden admiring
the strange and beautiful creatures as they passed,
never fully realising we were some of them.

Taylor was the main reason I was there. We had
met in a spiritual café some years previously and
maintained a strong yet sporadic connection during
our alternating times of need.

Taylor had a big heart and a pure soul, loved
poetry and cried at violin solos. His friend Mark
was more abrasive, loved a good intellectual
(sometimes even physical) sparring match. Anna,
who was to me a new and ever so friendly face, was
softly spoken, flinched at the touch of another and
carried a tiny bag in which she could just about fit a
Mary Poppins-style expanse of treats inside.

Today there was only one special on the
proverbial menu, which we took turns sniffing off
the backs of our fists. The subject turned to
censorship.

"All of my jokes get banned from print" Mark
complained, having submitted a number of
supposedly humorous books to various disturbed
literary agents.

"That's because they're all about the Jews!"
Taylor suggested helpfully.

"You can't say anything anymore!" the wannabe
comedian complained. "I feel as though I'm a part
of a marginalised group myself: people who can
take a joke."

"It's healthy to have boundaries," Anna
interjected. "There's too much violence and
prejudice in the world already."

"You may call it 'violence and prejudice'. I just
call it the truth," Mark added defensively.

"The truth is subjective, we all know that. There
are consequences to the messages being circulated,
so they may as well be dishonestly uplifting. Do
you want everyone to kill themselves? No, more art
should be banned. Particularly if it's been made
recently. I went to a modern art exhibition once
which had a pile of toilet rolls in a glass case. I
mean, spare me! That level of malicious
incompetence shouldn't be permitted," Anna trailed
off as Mark re-stocked her hand.

People nearby knew exactly what was going on,
but by intervening they would only have rendered
themselves hypocrites. The rebellion was
infectious; bolshy individuals approached the table
in order to enquire about the possibility of joining
the fun, but mostly no one cared: it was almost as
though there were more pressing global issues than
trying to impede those enjoying themselves.

Some may have felt it was wrong to have a good
time while our more distant brothers and sisters
perished through war, hunger or disease. However,

after several discussions on the matter I had concluded that it was my duty to source elation wherever I could find it. It was rare that euphoria was even an option for me, but today was a blessed opportunity to expand my emotional horizons.

As a result of the abject indifference displayed by those around us the scene went on unamended for several hours before the four of us decided to go back to Taylor's flat.

As we were leaving Taylor opened the door for a bustle of ladies and we were approached by a devout religious pilgrim looking out of place in the modern world. Buzzing like fridges, we tried to make it clear that now was not the right time.

"But perhaps it is," the zealot retorted silently.

"Have you ever thought about the meaning of life?" the devotee ventured outwardly, perceiving himself to know the response to every answer that could follow.

"Oo, I know this one!" Mark sensed a welcome confrontation. "It's Jesus! Now leave us alone," he uttered cruelly.

"Do you know what His two greatest commandments were?" the pious man continued on a lonely quest for an uplifting spiritual exchange.

"Now this one's much harder. Let me hazard a guess: 'Do what I say before I smite you!' and 'Go to Hell if you don't believe I exist'?" Mark was feeling particularly confrontational, as if this gentle man was a boulder between himself and Earthly delights. But, despite the tough crowd, the young believer continued. Perhaps nothing was too tough in his eyes for his God.

"Jesus's two greatest commandments were firstly to love the Lord your God with all your heart, soul, mind and strength. Secondly: to love your neighbour as yourself." The man-child seemed visibly proud of himself.

"Would you love me enough to leave me alone? What are you trying to achieve here, harassing us like this? What could possibly drive you to such a thing?" Mark spat.

"I only desire to praise God all of my life and put the world to rights," the servant of Christ said after a brief pause.

"I don't understand you," Mark clarified.

"In my way of looking at life Jesus has established the goal posts. Everything else is just a folly or distraction."

But it was too late: the young Christian's conversational sparring partner shook his head in exasperation and walked off into the pitch black of night lit only by artificial light.

Mark then went to catch up with the rest of us for we'd already vacated the scene of the accident, the age old collision between the faithful and faithless.

"Never have I met someone so devoted to delusion," Mark said to me, exasperated as he skipped towards a precarious future. Someone was wise in a world of fools, I thought. However, the lines between the two were notoriously blurry.

Chapter Four

Once I had returned to Cambridge I soon found that I was as disappointed by codeine as I had been with crack. Several times now I'd tried what I had been told was a suitable amount, but maybe I'd been mistaken about the dosage or else had been sold some bad gear because the only perceivable result of ingesting this oh so promising substance was a pernicious itching sensation which occupied my entire consciousness.

If I had been sold some dodgy stuff once again I had no right or inclination to question my man: the trouble I would potentially incur would only distress me further.

Instead I ventured once more into another still, cold night inspired by my friends' invitations to dance. I cared not for the day, which I had slept away in order to avoid the incessant scratching that accompanied my every waking moment.

"In order to find the God that made women, we have to stop following the God that men made," I said in conclusion to a long and winding rant about the need for female role models. It encompassed a range of subjects from the shameful lack of rape condemnation in The Bible to false religion and the real role of Mary Magdalene in Christ's inner circle.

I then sensibly resigned my brash attempts at interacting with random passing strangers and instead hit the dancefloor. I started to move, my curves melting into a song I'd never heard before but somehow seemed familiar.

The pill I had taken in the queue an hour ago while standing in the pouring rain wishing I had never came had begun to take effect. The first change sensed was the sheer warmth of the room as I got through the door: an electric pleasure shot through me which I felt I had no right to experience.

It was as if my deity had finally heard me when I said I needed a lift and obliged with the hit of all hits, a beam of ecstasy straight from the heavens: I felt temporarily illuminated by my love for life.

While trying my best to groove to each swiftly changing tune I presented all the grace of an elephant falling down the stairs, but I didn't let that stop me. I loved to express my emotions in all kinds of ways; dancing to music whether alone or in crowds seemed the perfect solution to unexpressed feelings. I liked all kinds of genres from bombastic classical pieces to the formative years of hip hop. So long as it was respectful and uplifting it was my jam.

Swaying, sweating and swearing with delight, I did not have to exert myself in order to create youthful memories I would always recall with glee.

The next day I awoke in a different frame of mind. I switched on the television to try to distract myself from the pristine white snow of a new low.

Onscreen a love story had reached its climax as the monologue began to play. The two lovers were completely entwined, with the young woman looking up helplessly at her amour as he confronted her with a parade of wisdom:

"You think you don't deserve me, but you do. You place me so above you, but all I need is to be right beside you. You believe you'll always love me, but you won't. You see me as the only one you'll ever want, but you're wrong."

I switched the stations, but finding the alternatives worse I soon switched back to watch them continue their intense intellectual sparring:

"I've got the keys to real, meaningful change," she said.

I watched keenly, but her supposed lover didn't even flinch.

"Doesn't that scare you?" She squealed, losing all semblance of self-control.

He soon found the words to put her in her place:

"You're completely mad, boring and stupid, but I love you. You smoke like the scorched Earth, drink like a whale and devour each experience as if it was all for sale.

"But don't ever leave me thinking of you too many years later, sat upright in bed like a ghost has come visiting in the night. Don't make me have to remember your bright, dove-like eyes with their sneer of condescension. I don't want to know all your excuses for treating me the way you do, but it will suffice, I guess, if you would only give me one or two."

I decided that, although I desperately wanted to, I could not follow the plot and turned the television off in order to start into motion the doldrums of the day. I went downstairs to find my Mum washing up with great reluctance. In glancing round at her beloved only child the matriarch soon realised something was wrong.

"Did you take something last night, Clara? You don't look right."

Having forgotten to check the mirror, I immediately felt sick.

"I don't disapprove of drug use, I just think it comes with dangers. Much like loving someone. Be careful, won't you. I've seen the news about the youngsters who after taking one pill – half a pill, even – never return home."

At the conclusion of such a disastrous interaction it was all I could do to dress quickly and vacate the house, preferring to walk alone in the fields in a bedraggled state rather than face the judgments for and consequences of my actions.

Chapter Five

Among the various acquaintances scattered around me, I found that Carl's friend Karen was a particular hoot. Anal sex was something Karen had a taste for and she loved it so much her passions had rendered her almost incontinent at the best of times. Still, she could not control herself and embarked upon a series of love affairs to satiate her desire for this most sinful of practises.

Other friends found it more funny than shameful; apparently every time Karen ran to the toilet there would be fits of laughter to accompany her bowel movements. She tried her best not to join in with them, but the situation – not to mention her arsehole – seemed beyond repair and laughter was always the finest of medicines, anyone could tell you that.

Karen feared the kind of old age which awaited her given the state of her body at 32, but she tended to live moment to moment and did her best to ignore the warning signs of a darker future. Such was the attitudinal norm of the society in which she dwelt: no one had the answers to the big questions and morsels of wisdom and foresight were all any relatively young mind seemed capable of handling.

Despite my sporadic need for such company, I would also successfully avoid the Hell that was all fellow humans in order to sit in the corn fields near my humble family home. I was not alone: I had brought a copy of my poetry collection with me, 'The Sun Of Understanding', and perused it as the largest of all the heavenly bodies in my vicinity glowed an amber orange just above the horizon.

I had written hundreds of poems by that point, which was inherently better than none. After all, a life devoid of poetry was not a life worth living and, despite the fact that I'd only sold about ten copies of this release, the scattered compliments I had received in response coupled with a sense of deep connection made my soul soar with pride. I continued to refresh my memory of my own words and ventured onwards deep into the heart of the book.

Weatherman

Oh no, the rain is coming down
It's falling hard now all around.
It stirs the monsters in your head,
Makes you awake and sit up in bed.

Look now, the sunshine never ends
While you make darkness your best friend.
Go out and enjoy some piercing rays
To burst the bubble of isolation.

In time the wind will speak your name
Throughout the back streets and the main:
Avenues of deep understanding
Filled with blessed noise.

And when the mountains become dust
You will know surely who to trust:

Fake gods and real scoundrels
Traipse across the deserts of your mind.

As I came to the end of my collection of hybrid thoughts I found myself wondering what it all meant. Did these ideas offer anything to another or was that nothing but an egotistical assumption? Nevertheless, I continued to reach out with words to my abstract audience: writing was my greatest ally.

After completing the inspection of my short poetic offering I went home in a slightly more thoughtful state of mind than when I had left the house and could only assume this to be a good thing: progress was mine, temporarily at least.

Chapter Six

As far as my close friends went, Johnny Fox was the closest. Our introduction had taken place in Mill Road cemetery in 2010, where I was paid to walk dogs at the time. I had bad dreams after disturbing the graves with my footprints, but little did I know that my whole life was to become a bad dream for nearly a decade from that point onwards.

Johnny always told me pride was my deadly sin, but I feared I exhibited more than one. While tidying the bedroom of his flat on Mill Road after a particularly heavy night, stained brown tin foil strewn around the place, our mutual friend Leo spoke to me about the finite nature of all things.

"Everything will vanish one day and be washed away by the corrosive sea of time." He paused before looking me straight in the eyes with a serious sense about him. "Even your book."

"Oo I have a funny feeling you're trying to hurt me," I replied honestly.

"I'm not trying to hurt you, I swear!" Leo lied.

"Haven't you heard the Yeats line: Tread softly because you tread on my dreams?"

Leo had not; I thought him a malicious fool, a stealer of dreams and a downright snake. I would soon be proven correct, of course, but for now it was merely a dull gut feeling.

Years later Leo told me his Dad had died in a car accident and, though my other friends didn't believe him, I was naive enough to lend him £20. Then another £30. Finally an extra £20, making a grand total of £70. On the day Leo said he was getting paid and would repay the debt fully he stopped answering his phone.

The last phone call I had with him he was slurring his deceitful promises in an intoxicated state and I perceived my quest for repayment to be a lost cause. There was to be no recompense and our friendship suddenly slid into the abyss of the past, as he had predicted it would.

Still, some relationships lasted and I was grateful for them. There were the many lovers who had in time become friends along with school chums whom I would never see again. Most relationships were predominantly maintained through technology anyway, no matter what their nature.

One day I heard that a bitter old failure of an alpha male had burnt 'The Sun Of Understanding' in front of a couple of mutual acquaintances. It became clear that some men didn't much tolerate ambitious women and in fits of jealousy would try to tear creatives such as myself - and my flowery dreams - down.

In the aftermath I was reminded of something memorable Johnny had once said in order to fight the demons of my fretting: "Some people struggle. Some people fly. But always remember those who fly will struggle and those who struggle will one day fly. The best thing to do, if you are in a stationary position, is to admire others as they soar."

If only certain others would take such advice, I bemoaned as I watched the flying mocked and attacked in jealous fits. My initial response to Johnny's words, however, somewhat blunted his sense of his own profundity.

"There are very few admirable birds in the cultural skies these days. Those who do spread their wings are in danger of being shot down!"

I often found in attempting anything at all one was inviting criticism from all quarters, but my dear friend would not be swayed by my negativity.

"Then admire someone you know. Admire me!!"

"Are you flying high?"

"Always!" Johnny confirmed his truth with a sweet smile.

Yet few really listened to Johnny, preferring their ways of competition and sin - voices of wisdom became lost in the wind.

I didn't understand why certain men would react in such ways to my heartfelt literary output. In my pondering I struck upon unanswerable questions: when did men start hating women and why? This was as futile as asking why the world turned and I could not bring myself to truly dwell upon an answer lest it bring me too much sorrow: a melancholy I could scarcely afford would strike me on occasion, but for now it was sleeping.

Chapter Seven

One afternoon in Johnny's flat the conversation drifted, as it inevitably did, towards politics. There had been another mass shooting in the United States of America, though the details of the news and whether the victims were children, minorities or the religious blurred in my wholly intoxicated mind as joints were passed and powders were snorted in turn.

All I knew was that someone had lost their life today; someone vulnerable, something pure. All of this in the plural. It was almost too much to contemplate and I was grateful for the blurring of my perception.

"So basically Americans killed most Native Americans and now they're killing their own children. Not to mention all the other countries they've attempted to dominate through the years. Serious, fundamental questions need to be asked and the American Dream needs to at least evolve," Matt, the newcomer to the scene, remarked.

Smoke drifted and hung in the air, dissipating with each passing figure as we shuffled around the room making tea and sourcing other such nourishing resources.

A question came to my mind and amidst the crowd I turned to my mate Dave. I almost whispered it as though I was saying something questionable or even racist, but in essence it was innocent enough: "Dave, what do Americans want?"

Dave laughed and replied decisively: "Everything!" I thought it ever so profound, dwelling on this verdict as if examining the evidence.

Politically speaking, I was radically left wing. I took a test online to find out where exactly I sat on the political spectrum and the results declared I was so far to the left that I waved farewell to my nearest ally, Karl Marx, before almost falling off the map.

Indeed, I was the ultimate sharing, caring, tax the rich, animal welfare prioritising, anti-war, pro-abortion and equal rights advocating Loony Lefty. In other words I was in many senses the antithesis of Hitler, which was objectively no bad thing. However, I sure got my share of shit for my 'hippy' viewpoints.

Anyone would think fascism was back in fashion in Brexit-ing Britain: as a result of a resurgence of nationalism and a Tory government seemingly permanently flirting with extremism, the constantly spinning attitudinal wheel had once again turned to the dark side; the historical horror and bloodshed of far right ideology had all but been forgotten by a new generation who selectively saw only the harsh appeal of cultural discipline and the sinister harmony of strictly enforced social order.

Following the emotional low of contemplating the incessant gun violence in the States, my inner world migrated to the subject of beliefs. I decided that I believed in everything: God, love, Jesus, angels, karma, reincarnation, fairies, ghosts... All of it mingled in a great melting pot of plausibility.

For, yes, I found it hard to doubt. If someone had once said it was so why should I not believe them? Were others not trustworthy? Just because I hadn't been to Fiji didn't mean Fiji was merely a rumour.

I concluded I had great trust in my fellow humans in some ways, but absolutely none in other senses: I couldn't trust my best friends with my sensitive feelings, let alone anything physical. In time they would mostly morph into enemies, but that was another story.

For now we were embroiled in superficially stable relationships with each other; some sexual, some not. Jessica mostly scored Class As and had a series of dubious relationships with questionable characters. I wrote my deepest, most poetic feelings down at length to an audience of up to three. Jules tried to sleep with anything that moved except women with short hair. If they had grey hair, though, that was magnetic. Them's the rules, no one said they made sense.

It occurred to me that most of the people I knew were singing from the same hymn sheet: the forgotten souls wondering when they will be remembered, the downtrodden hoping one day to rise.

Namina, Johnny's upstairs neighbour in their block of flats, had no interest in their goings on. The only occasions she intervened were when the acoustic guitar came out.

"I can hear you through the floor!" she would scream on the doorstep, completely devoid of grace, taste or dignity.

"It's only an acoustic!" I protested as Johnny roared expletives in the background; being the youngest party to feature in the disagreement I was playing the mediator as well as I could.

Wishing all the while I had an electric to really jar proceedings, I made my excuses and played quietly. Then, when the beauty of the melodies and cadences suddenly struck me akin to lighting or the blow of a boxer, I'd lose control and sing heartful songs of victory and defeat at the top of my lungs.

I struggled in observing the mental health of our species at times like these. How individuals within a (sane or insane) society stay sane is one question for the mind. How sane a society is collectively is another line of thought. Where was the sanity to be found if music couldn't be welcomed?

I had met people like Namina before. "All music sounds the same to me: it's just noise!" a mathematician from Cambridge University had told me madly many years previously. It had always stuck in my mind as a polaroid moment of abject ignorance. I thought about the statement for the entire time I babysat the man's two children. So Mozart sounds the same as The Beatles, he says? Just noise, he says! Mind-boggling.

I had matured to live by the maxim that if you've never had a complaint from your neighbour about playing music too late or too loud you're not a real music fan, but if you've had more than one complaint you're disrespectful. I eventually tried hard not to distress Namina further as a result of my internal debates on such matters.

Chapter Eight

I coldly avoided my mother and once again stayed round Johnny's place, sleeping in the spare room as I regularly did. In the early afternoon I awoke with a fervent sense of confusion.

"Morning, Johnny. How are we?" I spoke with a gravelly voice, igniting an artificially pleasant conversation which I would soon completely derail.

"Well, I'm fine, thanks. How are you?" Johnny whispered through the hazy room.

"Freaked out and fucked up," I confessed.

"Sit down, there's a smoke here and the kettle's just boiled. Tell me all about it?" Johnny's reply soothed an emotional open wound.

"It's the world, Johnny. It's such a mess. I was raised on Disney and Little House On The Prairie: I wasn't prepared for a society riddled with rape, violence and hatred."

The rant went on for hours. But Johnny was there through it all, weaving in wisdom from his childhood and various spiritual excavations with the aura of Gandalf incarnate.

Johnny and I even had matching Lord Of The Rings jewellery which we wore on our fingers and would do a first bump with sporadically along our journey together. We felt entwined for a moment as lovers of spirit, not flesh; Johnny saw my inner light beyond the seemingly cloudy exterior.

One thing could be agreed upon, though, after extensive existential debate: Time + people = awful things.

Later that evening when I was alone in Johnny's spare bedroom I found myself messaging Taylor once again. He wanted to call, but I refused the suggestion by explaining: "It's dead quiet this end of things, the kind of silence which should not be broken."

Every moment was my muse and I contented myself by writing poetry.

Spiritual Shipwreck

Deep at the bottom of the sea of life
There lies a wreckage called My Soul.
Far beyond all fish and fins
Ghosts' faces never grow old.
Most don't believe it exists,
Haunted by past incarnations and grandiose
moments.
But I know its every secret,
And how safe it is from surface storms.

Despite being able to count literature among my more reliable sources of contentment I was torn in many ways, most essentially between blissful ignorance and informed panic: was engaging with the horrors of the world healthy or was a sense of detachment necessary in order to persevere?

I would debate these dilemmas endlessly, tying myself in anxious knots of uncertainty: to care with all my heart may render it broken, yet to care not at all I would have to stop my pulse.

This seemed a dangerously appealing option at times as the sense of external rejection and internal torment fuelled my fleeting desires to die.

However, at that point in time the pain I would evoke in those I would leave behind alarmed me more than my own distress at remaining and so long as that ratio remained I could not in good conscience invite a premature ending to my troubled story.

Onwards I marched into bleak tomorrows, bruised and battered by the storms of the past. The notion of suicide surrounded me evermore as I observed it in our collective behaviours and decisions, but having identified a self-inflicted death as my enemy I fought long and hard to cherish my existence.

Despite this inner steel, in between my parties and good times I had committed multiple infidelities in my monogamous relationship with sanity. I self-harmed, nearly got sectioned and began smoking as a teenager in order to attempt to prematurely end my life in a socially acceptable manner.

I distracted myself from such woes through writing.

If the answer to the meaning of life really is 42, what is 43 then? Wrong? Or something more?

Are you looking for something? If so, what is it? Can you find it at the bottom of a bottle of wine, at the end of a white line or through the eye of a syringe needle picked up off a dirty floor? Can you find it in the bluebell fields while tripping on shrooms, water caressing your tanned legs as you wade on through the river bed; standing on the muddy banks, do you survey your kingdom of all that is while starting to question the root of such bliss? Can you find it through meditation or prayer? Can you find it everywhere?

I hoped one day to write a novel, but the nature of the task seemed overwhelming at that stage. I didn't even have a title! No, my need for creativity was temporarily satiated by lone passages such as these and the poems that followed flashes of inspiration as night follows day.

Chapter Nine

Phil, a friendly neighbourhood face, suddenly made an announcement on a rainy Sunday at Johnny's place.

"I'm 30 tomorrow. I'm wondering at what point do you see things clearly and know what you're doing? Do you know what you're doing, Clara?"

I was sure as soon as he directed his gaze to me that I most certainly did.

"Yes, I'm following my intuition. My emotional radar guides me every step of the way. But that's all I know."

"Every step of the way to what, though?"

I thought deeply for a moment, felt a sense of dread, and concluded that I had no real answers: I had spoken my modest portion of truth already.

I shrugged. "We're all heading towards extinction, really. But we must do our very best to live our idiosyncratic dreams and not uniform nightmares. The nature of our journey dictates the destination to some degree: we've just got to love the people around us and try the best we can."

"Learn and grow!" Johnny piped up with his seemingly lifelong catchphrase, used liberally in a variety of situations. He must honestly believe in these words if he said them so often, I had long ago concluded.

And why not? Learning and growing was what all healthy life forms did. The numerous plants in the front room grew towards the rays of the Sun, the dogs that visited obeyed their owners. So too must humans grow towards and obey their need for love itself, I believed; it was as natural as breathing.

I had never been a great communicator as I could navigate the depths much better than the surface, but my pressing need to connect meant I was forever embroiled in interactions with varying degrees of success.

Hating the forced nature of cut-and-paste conversations involving the weather, sports or television I would often rather abruptly introduce more dangerous topics without warning. Interrupting was also a problem: verbal patience was a virtue I was yet to attain.

Still, no one could call me abrasive. It was more a pressing need for spiritual progress which pushed me forward towards a precipice of understanding I felt constantly to be approaching.

If I ever did have a moment of real clarity and revelation it would ironically usually be when I was at my most intoxicated. An epiphany would arrive, yet I would forget it or be unable to write it down and the insight would pass despite being remembered in some part of my being. Even if I did make it to the stage of recording such a vision, how would I possibly phrase it? Such moments seemed ineffable in their mystery and were preserved only in my deepest soul.

Despite such fleeting senses of clarity I looked at my friends sometimes, my very life even, and wanted to run. There were too many incidents I didn't feel comfortable sharing, too many lows I found myself having to emotionally navigate my way out of. I was drowning, not waving in most of my interactions; if my life was a novel it would rightly have been banned.

Still, I could not help but feel that breaking down any evident barriers between myself and others was The Key: the one way I could rid myself of this pain was to put it into words. And besides, I considered internally one rainy Thursday, "if the truth can't be published I don't want to write."

In many ways this was an understatement because if the truth couldn't be accepted I had no desire to live. This was the undercurrent I had yet to perceive, though I sensed it all about me: the lies, hypocrisy, deception and sneaky behaviour of my fellow humans disturbed and dissuaded me from the path I was in the midst of travelling. It wasn't just the politicians, it was the people who voted for them. It was the empathy the general public showed duplicitous individuals and their demonic need for influence. Blessed are the meek, but cursed are the power-hungry, I had concluded long ago.

Despite a passionate desire to connect with others I was often uncomfortable externalising my inner experiences and felt in doing so I would perhaps commodify my very existence; I was not selling a product, I was promoting truth.

Sometimes I hurt people through the expression of my deepest feelings and at other points I felt the need for duplicity in order to avoid confrontation. Given my relative youth, my desire for acceptance remained remarkably strong, but mine was a soul just yearning for release.

When I couldn't find it through words I tended to turn to more illicit means of escape from the suffocating clutches of the mortal realm.

Chapter Ten

Fights in my family home were akin to watching
The Beatles phenomenon unfold in the 60s: people
were happy to scream, but they weren't capable of
listening. Following several days of illegal raves
and adventures I returned to face the fury of my
mother.

"You've got to think of the future, Clara! It's no
use ending up like me, burnt out and broken. I want
you to have something better!"

I was in desperate need of recovery and to find
instead a confrontation awaiting in a perceived
place of solace was almost too much to bear.

"The future? The future is fatal. We all know
that, Mum. It's day-by-day living for me right now;
I like to live in the moment and take each second as
it comes. I might not be accomplishing much, but
Lord knows I'm trying. I'm sorry that's not good
enough for you!"

With doors slammed and harsh words hanging
in the air we both slept uneasily, our respective
thoughts consumed by worries of what was to
come.

Throughout it all I lived by one motto alone: you
get what you give, you lose what you steal. Most of
the young souls around me fought against the
karmic laws of existence, swimming against the
tide of love or thieving their ways to temporary
success. I decided to submit to the forces of
spiritual development which I knew deep down
governed all things.

Indeed, I often felt myself to reside in the arms of the universe, a tiny speck in the grip of a giant force incapable of deception or lies: we were all given our allotted portion of blessings according to our thoughts, words and deeds - at least that's what I believed.

My lovers rarely showed any understanding of this – and, therefore, me. Instead they would berate me for giving change to the homeless while simultaneously taking all they could energetically and physically source from me. "They'll only use it to buy drugs," my date for the night, Sean, said when I dared to show generosity to a beggar. He was blind to both the nirvana and madness of acute perception, seeing little or nothing of the truth of love that surrounded him.

I didn't give a shit what the homeless spent my money on: I merely wanted my fellow human beings to be happier. Yet all I saw was misery and the misdirected blame for it. I perceived Earth to be a lowly place, seemingly in the throes of mental illness – inhabiting this planet was at times barely preferable to oblivion. But it was my world and I felt obliged to try to help those who were struggling.

It became apparent at times that everyone in my troubled life was going under or fighting not to. As the years passed, so the list of those loved and lost extended. Whether they vacated this world through drug overdoses, suicides, accidents or violence every one was missed by someone.

A shout out to all the souls departed and those

who think of their lost loved ones daily, the memories drowning out the ability of the living to focus on the present as though a part of their spirit had detached. Maybe it would never return.

In the face of the loss, despair and existential crises I marched onwards into the great unknown, tomorrows spread out before me as a blanket strewn with broken glass.

All those I thought I'd be friends with forever would soon fall into the past, transitioning from people I truly loved into arch enemies without putting up so much as a hint of a fight. No calls late at night, no stray emails in my junk folder begging for forgiveness and no acknowledgement of the efforts I had made with these wayward individuals for most of my twenties.

How was I supposed to know how little I ultimately meant to those around me during those crazy years? I had no clue until it was too late and regret consumed me whole.

Sometimes, when I was alone with my dreams, I cast my wishes into the great well of our collective consciousness: I wanted to be safe, loved, healthy and happy and prayed for these things daily. These were fleeting emotions as yet, but I hoped that would change.

Chapter Eleven

"This system of things has to go. Working for 70 years to earn a pension before you die is a formula which only works for the 1%. The rest are just economic cannon fodder, treading water or, if successful, climbing on the backs of their brothers and sisters to get ahead. We have everything we need to have a better world, we're just not choosing it," Johnny opined one dull and rainy Sunday.

"Sharing is something every parent teaches their children, but greed too often results," I agreed, contemplating the sinister rainbow of problems that we humans had created for ourselves. The green of injustice, the yellow of inequality, the purple of stupidity; all blended together to make a quite repulsive sight no one truly wanted to dwell on.

We drank our wine and smoked our joints, pretending life was somewhat a party. But the pain in our souls and the alienation from the norm were taking their toll on our moods.

Depression was all too common in my world: suicides, slow and fast, permeated my understanding of life. It was all I could do not to join the morbid procession of those inviting an early death.

Johnny's was a more joyous and ebullient soul, though, greeting every recognisable face that passed as he strolled the streets he had made his own and wishing them well on their respective quests. He was a popular man, a legendary artist in Yorkshire and a raver of some reputation.

Being an older man - no one could agree on his exact age - he told tall tales of Carnaby Street in the 1960s, Syd Barrett and his guitar playing at house parties and the torture of growing up in the archaic middle class. Johnny was a proud commoner now and considered the latter term a prize rather than an insult.

As well as listening to Johnny's words of anarchic wisdom, I continued to learn so much from writing.

Ye Eternal Pilgrim

When dreams overleap themselves
And sanity escapes the mind,
When your best laid plans lead to Hell
And Heaven within is hard to find,
If all about you are in chains
Yet criticise your freedoms,
And in dissecting their foul politics
All that you see is a lack of vision,
If loneliness is your best friend
While others are more dubious,
Then you will find the soul a guide,
Ye eternal pilgrim.

In externalising my deepest loves and fears I could somehow identify life's important moments and consider the best ways to deal with them.

What I found when I looked inside was that I fundamentally had a polarised sense of myself: part of me was ever so confident that I could change the world and the other part wasn't confident that I could walk in a straight line without tripping. With such incongruous inner workings those crucial points in life which make or break one's future were tricky.

Keeping calm during these sacred incidents, these twists and turns on life's pathways, was a superpower in my mind: when the world was falling down all around you could your emotions remain allies or would they betray you, leaving you bereft and devoid of all hope?

I had embarked upon a series of senseless romantic relationships during my younger years. Some led to sordid sexual encounters, others led to heartbreak, one led to an engagement; in different ways they had all ultimately led to nothing.

Sometimes I found the need for connection overwhelming. One or two of my teenage lovers had struggled even to speak English, let alone evoke intrigue and romance. In these instances I felt silence led to Heaven, but talking raised Hell. Physical connection was accomplishable while mental union remained horribly out of reach.

Being a sapiosexual creature such dalliances didn't last long. After having remained on the outskirts of true love for many years, I now yearned for the centre of the storm.

I had fundamental faith in the goodness of my very soul, that whatever strife may come or dreams be dashed, mine was a heart worth loving. I just had trouble meeting people who agreed with my self-assessments, that's all.

Apart from my consecutive lovers, I also held a series of lowly positions of employment which I was equally uninterested in. Cafes, restaurants, shops, pubs. Whatever.

I was often fired or walked out of such roles. On several occasions I was told that my "heart wasn't in it." Whose heart was really in flogging watches or selling booze to alcoholics, though? I may not have had a direction in life, but that surely wasn't the right way.

I had no idea who or what I wanted to become, but time passed regardless of my decisions about it all. The combination of getting high and getting laid was pretty much a full-time vocation, anyway.

I had a naturally obsessive personality. It was healthy for me to be distracted by someone or something most of the time; it was the dispassion which worried me most.

Chapter Twelve

I decided to have an adventure and visit Taylor and his impressive array of friends in London. It was that time of year when spring greeted summer with open arms and Camden was alive with sunshine and characters. Taylor and his crew were no exceptions.

At some point in time Spacebass handed me a rolled delight filled with three types of h and a sprinkling - "a smattering" - of c. I ended up listening to music in the early hours, cherishing every song. Yes, I had made a playlist of my favourite tracks, but somehow each random choice seemed right.

"Oh, that reminds me of something I've forgotten," I said blearily at the height of the waves of euphoria: my conversational skills were punished by my inebriation.

I dwelt again upon the sensation of feeling that I was at the centre of all things and nothing at all simultaneously; mine was an earthly paradise just for a few fleeting seconds.

As soon as I had recovered from my latest sesh I set my creative mind to work and wrote a poem focusing on many subjects simultaneously.

Tomorrow

I know what tomorrow brings:
A cup of sugar with a spider in,
A hug from a girl covered in fake tan

When you have dressed in white.

As a lonely bride,
Waiting for company,
I sing the songs the sirens sing,
Hoping one day to meet someone
Who satiates my need for the Sun.

The burning rays of white hot love
Sow the seeds as Jesus does
Of faith, belief and hope for more,
Yet my mind is filled while my heart is sore.

I felt pleased by the result, but was never sure if my words would please another. Therefore, I didn't share my poem with a soul, but let it consume a part of my heart that night as a creeping shadow covers the land.

Appreciation for the creative process was what kept me going through the dark nights of the soul which peppered my youth. I didn't know I was in a tunnel, let alone that I could emerge into light. Yet reality relentlessly ripples onwards for both the genius and the fool and, after all, as a relative youngster tomorrows seemed mine to conquer.

One Monday I rose early as though the day was unlike any other and I had to capture all of it. I was wrong, and as each hour passed the frustration grew. I wanted something more from life, but knew not what it was. A person, a feeling, an experience I would be pleased to be a part of. None of it was forthcoming and I trundled on laden with regrets and trauma as most living beings learn to.

"Years of frustration laid down side by side" came the haunting voice from the stereo and I could only dwell on the lyrics wistfully as I digested the delicious sense of meaning and truth to the song. Music that meant anything to anyone was hard to come by these days, but the past was littered with sacred wisdom, I found.

When viewed from a distance I considered that almost everything could become romantic: who hummed the first melody or uttered the first prayer? When was the concept of God first leapt upon or the first peace treaty conceived? When did Jimi Hendrix first drop acid and what did William Blake, the great dreamer, dream? I wanted to know it all, but sensed that by doing so one would go quite mad.

Despite all of my extensive quests for knowledge I found that I could only hold a very few of life's lessons in my mind; still, a great deal of wisdom seeped from my ancient soul. Ultimately, if I knew anything - anything at all - I felt sure that I was a good person deep down, where it counts.

I often remarked that anyone who wasn't practising love didn't understand scripture. Conversely, those who read scripture sometimes seldom loved. It was undoubtedly a confusing world and the wayward religion I was devotedly practising reflected that clearly.

I was really just seeking to live a life of love, but trouble resided under every stone I was foolish enough to turn over. Perhaps it was best to simply be, I surmised in the midst of my tornado of torture.

I felt sad sometimes that despite life's long and arduous road, there was never enough time to find all the gold in the hills, all the dolphins in the sea or the beauty in all art. Life on the whole seemed painfully short and dauntingly long; death seemed at some times tempting and at others petrifying. Such were the conflicts of my idiosyncratic existence.

Each of us was alike, though: consumed by doubts one minute and having achievements dwarfed by our egos the next. "If you ever get close to a human you'd better be ready to get confused" opened the next song and the singer spoke to me in ways few humans had been capable of.

It's funny how music can dominate one's life, forming soundtracks to moments or even whole passages of time. Songs could be company for the lonely, providing comfort that others could not.

Music = Life

Music is life;
Even when it's twisted and dark,
Let the melodies soar.
It's gonna be alright.
Hear the notes you need to hear,
Sing the words you hold so dear.
Pirouette to the grave
Because no one will save us
Like the singers tattooed on our arms.

Chapter Thirteen

I found existence to be a cacophony of noise filled with indiscernible answers: everyone had the solution for some conundrum or other, but few were in agreement and all wanted to be heard.

Thus a din was created which sometimes gave me terrible headaches. I perceived myself to suffer from these painful physical afflictions after long bouts of drinking or too much time in the sun, but really it was because the radio frequencies were full of conflict and I was a walking spiritual aerial.

Meandering around in an ungrounded daze seemed to be my way. Some would call me "aloof" or query my overt sense of distraction, but most allowed the sensations of abject hopelessness to continue unabated in my character, not knowing what to make of such a gaping cavern in place of existential clarity.

Indeed, meaning was something I struggled - sometimes failed – to find. "The meaning is demeaning," I had once said to a friend on the way to another house party, though I had no real definition for the outburst and therefore did not know whether or not she even agreed with my statement. I was just making obligatory noises along with the rest of them as the time passed.

Only when I was alone and silence enveloped me wholly could I find meaning in the words I employed, carving purpose from disparate lyrics and sewing sentences together that rung with a visceral sense of truth which lightened my soul in expression.

In all honesty I generally wrote for no one but myself - that was precisely the way it should be, I would console myself by saying. It amazed me to discover some bizarre quirks of the English language, such as the differences between "stationary" and "stationery" or "ween" and "wean". The pitter-patter of wisdom lay in such discernments.

I was beginning to feel as though life was a game played against a deity more skilled than anyone could imagine. Only fools believed they had a chance of victory, particularly if they refused to play by the rules as was so often the case. The mortals' games ended prematurely: they underestimated their opponent until they were utterly defeated, using inferior tactics against a superior strategist. Eventually their humiliation became so total that they refused to engage further.

Others respected their opposition, cautiously executing their very finest moves with a nervousness about what would come next.

I, meanwhile, sat at the great board of existence in awe of my supposed nemesis: I was afraid to make a move that would do any less than impress, frozen as I was by the extent of my admiration.

Every piece I touched was swiftly captured and removed from the tapestry before me and I could only seek to learn the wisdom I lacked myself.

God had been playing this game for a long time, you see, while I was merely a wide-eyed beginner. I would need to play again and again to muster a challenge to the great master, to understand as the holy do, to hone vision and foresight, defence and attack, to be composed in the face of such ingenuity.

Even then, my time was short while God's was eternal. Ultimately, life seemed akin to a game no one could win, so I decided to read some poetry to distract myself from this state of affairs. I came across one that struck a chord.

Yours

To touch,
To hold,
To mould,
To guide
I am only yours.

Give me another half a chance
And I can make you whole.
Watch me turn the dull metals of your days
Into fiery gold.

Turn your face to brighter tomorrows
And leave the shady past
Where ghouls and goblins
Climb the walls of the palace of existence.

I know I hurt you;
I hurt too,
Perhaps a little more than you.

For your care puts to shame
The relaxation of the dead,
But my dreams must live outside my head.
And after all,
I'm yours.

The poem touched upon the difficult concept of belonging to another, which for good reasons many shied away from: freedom was a prized possession to those who savoured it and many considered the compromises love brought to one's life to be objectionable. Thus the breakdown of most marriages I had observed, but not all. Some seemed truly happy; whether they were or not was a private matter.

I then contributed another of my own humble offerings to humanity's poetic oeuvre and went to bed satisfied with my output for the day.

Unconditional Love

Unconditional love is a riddle
To which few know the answer;
Rare it is that we give without feeling depleted
Or take without the sting of greed.
One must journey through the desert
To lay claim to a foreign paradise.
What a tortured and enchanting pathway
We all have traversed,
From the screams at birth to the tears of joy -
And yet it continues...

Chapter Fourteen

I burst into Johnny's living room one sunny spring afternoon and announced an epiphany.

"Johnny, I think I need to take myself more seriously."

So we had a pow wow featuring tea and some slim lines of k until I felt sick and went to throw up the copious quantity of alcohol I had just ingested. As the evening became morning I also had a stark realisation that I had consumed £20 worth of smokes in one night, which was enough to drive anyone off the wellness cliff.

"But seriously, Johnny," I rejoined when I had returned in a more clear-headed frame of mind, "everyone always warns people about taking themselves too seriously. No one tells you that you don't take yourself seriously enough. Maybe this is my problem."

"Just the one?" Johnny cheekily quipped, but found my thoughts impacting his as dominoes in a long line of consciousness stretching back through the aeons: recorded thoughts continued to influence, unheard of theories were constantly on the cusp of externalisation; original expressed ideas were a marvel to hear. He treasured our friendship just a little more and gave me £20 to ease my financial woes.

The next day I was having an inner dialogue while horizontal on Johnny's sofa. "Intelligence is a slippery fish. The cleverest people can't boil an egg and the stupidest people run the world. The fish are useless at climbing trees and the birds are useless at sprinting. You can be academically bright, streetwise through experience or innately philosophical. All are pieces of a very complex and intricate puzzle."

Some objected to my chaotic lifestyle, others called me a lunatic; I knew I was a child of God. Yet to many my actions and behaviours seemed strange, peculiar and bizarre: I was an original in a world full of moulds.

At times it seemed that only Johnny saw the Goddess in me, but he had eyes where others had gaping holes; he may have been almost alone in honouring my inner deity, but that made our connection so much more precious.

"Men may make up half of the human race, but many of them seem half-human," I confided to myself eventually after years of observing in horror as the behaviours and ideologies of the less fair sex dominated life.

I was almost constantly navigating the affections and requirements of males, from shaving my legs to avoiding unwanted sexual advances. It was an uphill task: the institutions I was so often coerced into being a part of and the societal norms I would be forced to adhere to had all been established by men.

Most religions were patriarchal by nature and viewed women in a demonic light despite the fact that most war, rape and crime was carried out by men. Where was the religion run by women which declared men to be subhuman liabilities? I had read feminist literature which proclaimed as much, everything from Valerie Solanas to Simone De Beauvoir, but in terms of the mobilisation of feminist concepts the world seemed a desert.

The Tories in the Houses of Parliament had almost banned truth from its doors: they were shocked and appalled by statistics and crime rates, but not by their own negligence. Meanwhile criminal activities went on within and without the board rooms of the powerful political elites; no one knew where the vicious circle had started or would end.

I concluded during my discussions with Johnny that women must take a long hard look in the mirror because whatever was being done to curb the male propensity to hate was clearly not enough. Sexism was everywhere from governments to religious scriptures to children's toys. Surely it was time for us women to get brave, find our voices and put misogyny in its place: the past?

Before our big fall out I talked to Leo about the level of toxic masculinity on show in the world.

"Men? I wouldn't piss on them if they were on fire," Leo had said while contorting his face into a grimace.

I found such attitudes interesting: though I believed passionately in equality I also found the occasional man who believed that women were generally superior in terms of their emotional fluidity and the competence of their faculties. I was never sure whether to argue the case for total equality or nod in tacit agreement as though I was being schooled.

Other inspirational men I had met lamented the lack of female leaders in the world and highlighted this imbalance of power as a problem.

For this conversation I had some regularly recited input: "Maybe if rape, domestic violence and femicide weren't so horrifically common and globally females were given access to education, reproductive healthcare and granted equal pay we could talk. Until then our hands are tied as bigoted men legislate our powerlessness and insist this was God's intention."

I would paraphrase such long-held opinions with more or less accuracy depending on my level of intoxication, but at least I knew my mind on this matter.

Despite England's supposed evolution in these areas compared to other regions of the world marital rape had only been made illegal in 1991. I found this fact to be a source of great national shame and thought of the subject of gender more often than many people seemed to.

I surmised that humanity as a whole was living in the dark ages with regard to sexual abuse and domestic violence, but what could I alone do about it?

The majority of people seemed to have their desire to stand out from the crowd - along with their self-esteem - corroded by the day. Blue was for boys and pink was for girls. Who dared argue and risk being ostracised while perhaps even going so far as to preserve the "they/them" pronouns of their offspring?

It was no life for me. I had known since I was eight years old that I did not want to reproduce. Perhaps it was the pressure I saw my parents under to both get along and provide for the family despite their characteristic make-ups mixing like oil and water? Again, I didn't know.

As a result of my contemplations and observations I felt scared for the future and for fellow females. The injustice was deafening. I decided then to read a book and find some words which could move me, teach me, make me feel alive. It took me only a few brief minutes before I found a gem to analyse:

"I am going into an unknown future, but I'm still all here, and still while there's life, there's hope." - John Lennon (December 1980)

This quote and its timing really struck me and I fell into a pool of depression for a prolonged moment. Was there to be no hope now that the man who spoke of it was dead, brutally murdered by someone who had previously requested an autograph and subsequently expressed no remorse? What kind of world had Lennon left? A voice told me it was a better one than when he arrived – perhaps that was the aim for all of us?

It was June 23rd 2016. Or was it the 24th? I couldn't give a fuck, but my favourite person at that point in time was due to come and visit soon, either way. Max used to be a musician before he sold Christmas trees. He had a terrific mind, which I just loved to explore, and during the course of the evening we eventually spent together I blurted out while I was drunk and overly friendly:

"I think you are a genius. I'm supposedly a genius too. A medium once told me and I was stupid enough to believe him."

I laughed and took another swig of rum and coke.

As we went on to discuss, geniuses are neither wholly mad nor rationally sane. They are a combination of the two. Their uniquely powerful intellects also tend to turn in on themselves, for though they can see what others do not, such an isolated experience and advanced state of mind could drive anyone mad.

However, after this conversation Max never spoke to me again. I still thought of him, though perhaps he was too sane for me. Crazy can be a good thing, unless it's not; that was a line I was clumsily navigating.

Another lover.
Where's my mother?
I just wanted someone to stroke my hair.
But oh no, full sex.
Horror, horror!
I just wanted someone to hold me for a while.

The following evening I found myself embroiled in an overly hectic schedule: another piss, another fag, another sigh. The night was closing in, collapsing as my lungs at times threatened to. Coughing and spluttering with a mixture of phlegm and blood emerging from my painful throat, I wondered at how old I had become at 28.

As I matured I realised that falling in love was bad for one's mental health. Though any wise owl could tell you that it had taken years of trial and error to reach this conclusion.

I had always dwelt upon the idea that, given our ongoing process of evolution, I should have perfected the art of falling in love by now, standing as I was on the precipice of the future.

Surely I should be able to display all of my best qualities as a peacock might reveal its stunningly intricate colours? But no. Instead all of my very worst traits came to the fore when I fell for someone and I would be left with nowhere to go except a deep inner pool in which to contemplate my own sordid reflection.

I'd had relationships in the past where each party seemed to mirror the actions and opinions of the other: hairstyles, sexual kinks, political opinions were all shared sooner or later. "Wherever you go, I go" seemed to be the implicit message - until there was nowhere left to go and our union came to an end.

That Friday some randomer from the States I'd met online messaged to say he wanted to visit, said he had a passport and had wanted to come to England since he was a kid.

"A passport and good intentions are a decent start to any adventure," I replied. But nothing came of it and our plans, as with the dream of human potential, slipped quietly into the past.

Wherever we were in the world each conscious individual had by now observed a quicksand of bad decisions the human race may or may not be capable of escaping.

Yet alongside the mistakes and sorrows the inescapable truth, I discovered in my overthinking, was that everyone would always be loved by someone. If it wasn't your mother, it was your lover. If it wasn't your pet, it was your God.

Sometimes it felt as if my deity was my secret admirer, giving me presents without gift tags: the air I breathed, the songs that lifted, the relationships that taught. Slowly, tentatively I felt myself to be discovering the source.

I loved it when I met people younger than me who went to church and engaged with their faith. It was almost as though the paedophilia, hypocrisy, misogyny, judgement, homophobia, closed-mindedness, cruelty, murder and warfare associated with religion had succeeded in putting the rest of the youth off. I felt drawn to outsiders, though, and no one was more marginalised in the modern world than the faithful.

Yet at the same time every human sin imaginable had been committed by members of the Church; rape, avarice, murder: clearly that's what happens when mere mortals are appointed to carry out God's work, I realised as I matured.

Some would say that the world was turning not burning, but they were a privileged minority ignorant of the suffering of the masses. Wherever I looked - religion, politics, economics - I saw only hardships and injustice.

It was bizarre to believe in God given such circumstances, but believe I did. I perceived my faith to be a sturdy vessel on stormy seas. However, I didn't much care for church: if you were going to move mountains you couldn't be confined to buildings. Furthermore nature was life's most powerful preacher, anyway. Instead I carried on as if Paradise was guaranteed and laughed at bumper stickers which said "Jesus Christ, save me from your followers!"

Politeness was also akin to another religion which I sporadically practised, but regularly deviated from as with all codes of conduct I encountered. I found that my devotion to manners made me a little morally neurotic, perhaps, but it was charming in its own way and I often received compliments on my civility from those who worked in hospitality; it was clear that holding similar positions had heightened my sense of equality.

Even at my young age I had loved God for an awful long time, yet I still sensed rightly or wrongly that God had loved me for longer. In being no fan of organised religion, I instead professed a kind of spiritual anarchy whereby every soul carved its own path using the wisdom it was exposed to. For example: some Christianity here, some Sufism there and a dash of scientific analysis. Perhaps such obfuscation was already the norm?

I considered life to be all about recipes. Some slept 12 hours a day while others felt fine on 8, some preferred multiple lovers while others were content with none, some liked a drink on a Friday night while others enjoyed a cigarette for breakfast. Each to their own, I thought. Everything in moderation, I learnt: most idioms perpetuated at least an inkling of truth.

Of course this process of spiritual enlightenment in which I partook required an agile mind capable of discerning truth from lies and wisdom from phatic bullshit. In my casual anthropological observations I had concluded that there didn't seem to be many of those about.

Nevertheless, I found it heartening that enlightenment had been attained by the Buddha through a mere 49-day meditation session under the Bodhi tree. It wasn't an unobtainable goal out of reach for the masses. It may take time, effort and focus, but on the contrary it was a state of mind all can - perhaps must - obtain.

The inner journey to such a spiritual destination was debatable, however, and one could only attempt to prosper given the materials and environments at one's disposal. I decided imitation of the masters was not the way forward, for every soul had its idiosyncratic nature and development.

Were Jesus, Buddha and all the great teachers that have ever been to have met they would surely have shared the love that they had found freely. However, that same love would have taken on differing forms given the alternate pathways each had taken to that very moment. Perhaps there would be laughter? Perhaps tears of jubilation would even flow?

Of course this daydream was an impossible mirage, for such beings only walked the Earth every millennium or so. Yet if more chose the opportunities life presented to them in order to evolve perhaps such pure-hearted vessels of the divine would appear with increasing frequency.

Who wants to be highly evolved given the struggles which accompany such mental transitions, though? People crucified Jesus then worshipped Him as the Son of God. Well then, what painful fates await the lesser mortals who seek His crown?

I enjoyed paraphrasing The Bible on occasion, particularly the message Jesus brought to His followers by saying "all this and more shall ye do." It was arguable whether the mere worship of Jesus was enough in His eyes or whether emulation was required.

I had been told of a mental illness called The Jerusalem Syndrome where sufferers have hallucinations involving Biblical figures or even believe they are some form of Messiah either before, during or after their visit to the Holy Land. Dark comedic sketches orientating around the madness of religion and the delusions which accompany belief were conjured in my mind upon hearing of such a condition.

Indeed, the sorrows and insanities which had taken place in the region that Christ called home since His time there could only reinforce the arguments of the atheists. As a comet leaves a trail of debris in its wake, so too had the world's most celebrated occupant left a legacy of torture, murder and suffering in His name.

Surely this was not as intended? Surely the divine messages had been mistranslated? While eating porridge I pondered such concepts, banality and profundity interwoven as always. Yet I could come to no solid conclusion and resigned myself to confusion as almost all must.

Though rowing strongly on the river of life, I lacked all sense of direction. The universe could be an unforgiving place when one was sloshed: gigs being missed or friends being lost forever were probably more plausible than gigs being savoured and friends being made forever. But twisted, broken people still had a right to the Sun.

Chapter Fifteen

"We'd make a terrible couple because I love you too much," wailed a lover on a radio play I was enjoying one sleepy Saturday as Johnny ventured out to shop for groceries and score.

"Every time I'm near you I go crazy. It's as though you are singing me a love song which I can't hear above the sound of my own screaming!"

This summed up something so perfectly about certain romantic entanglements I had sporadically experienced that I took a minute to digest the imagery. Love may well be the purpose of life, but madness so often follows. Yet going mad was not the purpose of life.

Indeed, most people seemed to be searching hard for sanity and finding only hints of what could be. Instead of perfect balance and harmony it was frequently the case that fools married the wise and sinners seduced the holy: seemingly nothing made sense in flesh nor spirit. How was a mind to cope?

I learnt long ago that I couldn't handle love: I wasn't used to it, hadn't been shown how to respond to it, never really understood that it could turn out well. I concluded that I was much easier to know if I didn't love you. If I loved you, look out because I would soon become a hot mess!

My behaviour when falling in love bordered on mental illness sometimes with some people. The messages I would send, the behaviours I exhibited, the feelings of obsession I had... None of it made any sense. It was all I could do to try to decipher these mistakes in my own time and put the pieces of my broken heart back together each time it shattered.

Still, if you've got one person in your life who loves and respects you no matter how awfully you behave, if you have one companion on the great journey of existence who would forgive the worst thing you've ever done, if you know the goodness of a single soul beyond this lifetime for sure, if you know one fellow existential traveller who couldn't do it without you then you are loved.

As it was with me and Johnny. We would spend days talking about the Roman invasion of Britain, the problems with academia and what we wanted to happen after we died.

We concluded nothing of any real substance, of course. Yet we both found our inquisitions had their own charms.

"What's the point of all this, Johnny? Breathing in and out, getting in and out of bed, moving in ever decreasing circles?"

"To learn and grow," Johnny said without missing a beat. He took a long, intoxicating drag on a joint and passed it to me after inhaling an inordinate amount of toxins. He thought for a while and then finally spoke, his words traversing the plumes of smoke between us.

"Did you know cigarettes contain more than 7,000 chemicals?" Johnny segued, and I shook my pretty head.

"What a bargain!" he quipped, hitting the conversational ball out of bounds. He chuckled too hard for too long at his own joke, but I still laughed the longest.

We continued on our journey to self-destruction, waving at achievement and success as we passed. Days would disappear in Johnny's front room, years if we let them. Hours slipped through our fingers as sand on a seemingly infinite beach. Whatever would be was objectively irrelevant, anyway. Why try to influence a pointless masterplan, if there ever was one?

No, it was best to declare yourself a failure before others could. Wanker, cunt, scumbag: I thought myself to be every conceivable insult and therefore rid myself of the pressing need for perfection.

I monopolised antisocial behaviours and upon awareness of a fresh wrongdoing I embraced it wholeheartedly. I knew I was a sinner, as we all were. But in my mind's eye I wasn't a bad person: I simply said "yes" too much.

Johnny was not a bad person in my opinion, either. In fact, in my eyes he was the best - he simply accepted everything and everyone without judgement. He would forgive the unforgiven and nurture the most pitiful thieves. He even had several deep scars to show for his troubles!

At this point in time the majority of people didn't seem to be sleeping so much as in fucking comas. Along with Sartre I considered Hell to be other people, certainly. But more specifically the kind of blind, superficial, vain narcissists which occupied most of the public sphere. I tried to stay out of it, though mainstream culture regularly intruded upon my senses and blurred my sense of self.

What does being normal entail, though? I'd never understood the rules and so refused to play the game. My piercings and tattoos marked me as an outsider, anyway. Yet I'd never attempted the dreads I admired on several of my dearest friends.

Chapter Sixteen

I burst into Johnny's living room one Friday night at what was supposed to be a time for a party, but I didn't feel in a suitable frame of mind for socialising: "I just had the worst pregnancy scare."

I explained to Johnny that I had taken the first test in a rush and, although it had at first seemed negative, I had returned from an adventure to find it seemingly changed to positive. I took a second test and it was a clear negative result, but the whole experience had put the fear of God into me.

"It's made me realise how vulnerable women are to having their lives overcome by male desires."

Johnny remained stonily silent, feeling himself to be in alien terrain to the male domain. The difficulty of such incidents was undeniable, yet I reasoned that there were no pauses on the journey to enlightenment: everything had a meaning, cause and effect. The most mundane moments could bring the most vivid epiphanies and striking realisations were followed by the dullest of days; the minute details of every second contributed to the splendour and horror of the whole.

The tricky part was finding a direction amidst the chaotic slew of experiences. I may not yet have known what I wanted to be, but I knew I wanted to be something worthwhile, to contribute to the society which had birthed and nourished me, to develop from a taker to a giver. I just hadn't been shown how.

I always thought that something would come to

me eventually, some revelation regarding the purpose of my existence. But years passed and despite the plethora of epiphanies regarding life, death and the in-between no vocation or means of stable income emerged.

The situation endlessly worried and frustrated my Mum, who had watched as her innocent and placid newborn had emerged as a temperamental young adult lacking any sense of purpose. Indeed, the human race itself seemed to be going through teething pains: I was simply one more wayward person in a troubled world.

It was almost impossible to see how things could change. Can anyone see clearly in a storm? Can anyone walk surely on uneven ground? How does a pathway to peace and prosperity emerge from a collective history seemingly dominated by theft, rape and murder?

It was difficult for me to find the courage to remain here, let alone hope for a better tomorrow. I did my best to stay afloat in rough seas; my soul my only compass, my God my surest guide, my mind my greatest enemy.

When the darkness overwhelms them and ghosts lurk in every corner of their minds, people should always remember the wisdom of their grandparents. So it was with me: my dear grandmother's words (spoken following my parents' divorce) reverberated in my head sporadically throughout those years: "You must make sure yours is a story of redemption."

The familial elder had obviously seen through

my forced smile to the collection of sorrows and regrets which already resided just behind it; she imparted some of the more precious words I had heard in my short life.

I was 19 when Grandma Mary passed away, but at least I had been really seen, heard and implicitly understood by someone at such a tender point in my life.

One of my good friends from the adult era of my life, Jessica, was seen years later with half her face sunken due to intensive drug abuse, drunk and slurring at a cashier in a local supermarket while clearly in need of a friend. Hers was not a story of redemption.

Still, neither of us was to know that during the midst of our friendship and onwards we had stumbled into the great unknown.

Chapter Seventeen

"Bodies turn to dust, but words never rust. They may move you, abuse you, hurt or confuse you, but they can always be rearranged."

I put down my pen, knowing I had communicated something worth saying and being satisfied - proud even - that I had at last done something right. I rolled a slim cigarette and smoked it to feel better, but only succeeded in feeling worse. Maybe 3 cigs before breakfast was too much - as with everything, I was still learning my limits.

When I was a child I had felt as though I stood inside a dream: the colours were vivid in every sunset, the wonder consistent in every sighting of a butterfly and the tastes of meals always incited noises of appreciation. I was never sure when these initial responses dissipated, but I more often than not awoke in a state of torment these days.

At what point life's intrinsic magic became tiresome was hard to discern, but some moments which could've hurt didn't and some experiences which shouldn't have scarred did.

The day my father walked out on my mother and me was particularly memorable. Having told me to "fuck off and ruin someone else's life" earlier in the day, by evening he had packed and left. I was 15 years old, on the cusp of adulthood, a young bird with a newly-broken wing.

When others love you madly you have a duty to love yourself, but when those closest to you love you only a little - if at all – the consequences can be devastating. It was not fair, but life so often wasn't in the short-term. Perhaps that's where my faith in long-term justice stemmed from: things must turn out fairly sooner or later if there was any point to living at all. Yet maybe this was another miscalculation to keep my others company. The good Lord knows I had emerged as a magnet for delusions.

Perhaps it was because I was a fey child, always feeling something special would happen to me; when nothing ever did it was inevitable that I would grow to be somewhat jaded.

Certain drugs were an easy escape from the overbearing nature of reality. Others forced me to confront emotions as physically as a bouncer, hauling me out of my comfort zone and into the emotional realms of the unfamiliar. I made footprints at times with great glee in the pristine white snow of my mind. I just was never sure which experiences would be which, what to expect on my psychedelic adventures, what would come next.

It was an eerie feeling, peppered with fear of the unknown. Of course one could mess with this sense of trepidation, attempt to gaslight oneself into certainty regarding the future. Yet always anticipatory anxiety remained a part of my life, an uneasy bedfellow with my obscure sense of pain.

Still, as long as I was at least high I considered myself relatively happy: the ice caps may have been melting, small children were being abused, governments were betraying those who voted for them, but I could always find joy in a bass line.

Indeed, I saw drugs as medicines; with them by my side I could converse with the gods and interrogate any ephemeral magic I came across. Aspects of myself emerged which I had no words to describe and, in threatening them with externalisation, found they too soon disappeared.

Meanwhile there were other thoughts and feelings that simply demanded to be freed from the cages of the human heart and mind - even soul. Telling the difference between thoughts which were best kept to oneself and those which would be gratefully received by the outer world was an artform I had yet to master.

Light humour in a dark world made the day worth living - Johnny was the source of most of the punchlines. At one point faeces were found in the middle of the front room, but Johnny claimed he couldn't confirm whether they were his or a visiting dog's. This made me laugh for a full minute when I heard and the cobwebs for a moment were shaken from my childlike heart.

My love for Johnny meant he could do no wrong in my eyes: I always knew he was trying his best even when he made the most vile mistakes.

His temper was a thing to be feared, though. In the mornings his rage was often audibly directed at one particular electronic device: his phone.

"YOU CUNT!! YOU FUCKING CUNT!!"

I initially thought it was an emergency, but after the second or third time I let him be. Morning rituals were different for different people: some practised meditation, others swore blue murder at their phones. Who was I to judge?

Chapter Eighteen

The next day I came across an impressive line while reading my beloved books: "God's plans are greater than our dreams."

I thought it profound with more than a hint of truth. Human fantasies can be so mundane: a new house, a new car, a new dress, a new lover. Yet the creator of the universe surely had real scope, vision and ambition.

I decided to add my own two cents to proceedings and wrote in my diary: "Faith in yourself is faith in your creator." Though it was now evening and I had slept the afternoon away, I was pleased with my output for the day. Indeed it reminded me of a kind of short riddle I had heard many moons ago: "If a man spends his whole life being lazy, never accomplishes anything and just before he dies poor and lonely he writes a line of poetry so beautiful it makes everyone who reads it cry, has he wasted his life?"

There were no right or wrong answers, but naturally thinking made them seem so. Most said that he hadn't wasted his life. Yet in observing wasted hours and futile quests for riches all around them those who reached that conclusion continued to be unaware of something potentially beautiful unfolding.

Instead of acknowledging the attributes the poet brought to the existential table the riddle became sanitised of wisdom and placed in a collection of interesting things someone once said rather than a message about patience and compassion.

It was impossible to truly waste a moment, I had decided long ago: after all, one's best ideas so often came when one was sleeping.

What was my excuse for troubling behaviour? "I'm not day-drinking and fucked-up: in fact, because being in tune with nature is important to me, I'm aligning myself with the trajectory of a downward spiralling planet. This is holistic living, baby!"

"Hippy logic at its finest," Johnny quipped.

Plenty of times I overdid it and didn't want to be seen in public. I laughed from a great height of highness at the pilgrims seeking to attain what I had found; I didn't know whether I was floating or falling.

It was precisely on one of these occasions when Johnny asked if I wanted to go into town. Initially I declined, saying "I would only walk around in a daze saying "look at the sky, it's so blue!" while you implored me to focus on the more pressing issues at hand."

I felt that level of disconnection from reality would be alarming to company, but Johnny had other ideas.

"Don't worry, I'll admire the sky with you," he said with the flash of a smile to treasure.

So that's what we did. Yes, the pollution struck me as an alarming eye sore and the colours blurred in my vision, but there were remarkable sights to behold simply by looking up.

I tried not to judge myself too much. After all

who had lived the perfect life? Was it Joan of Arc, burnt at the stake? Or Arthur Rimbaud, who left the world at 37? Was it Martin Luther King Jr., whose dreams brought his downfall? Was it George Best, taken too soon after years of alcoholism? Was it Jesus Christ, who cried out to God through His sense of abandonment?

I decided the best person ever had to be Keith Richards, who had long ago proved himself to be eternal. Yet it seemed this world was full of suffering wherever one looked, in great lives and humble existences. I didn't kid myself as to where I was on this hypothetical scale: a trip to the supermarket was an adventure for me. I mostly crawled from my bed to the pub on a good day.

On bad days I could lie in a comatose state for ill-defined periods of time undiscovered, turning over and over as though spiritual and mental discomforts were physical.

It's only when you're slightly away from events on the time-space continuum that you can rationally assess them and say "that was mad!" or "that was special!" So it was with me and the way I would meander through the days in a shambolic, bull-in-china-shop manner.

I had no idea what to make of the cards life had dealt me and could only deduce that I would have to try to make it to middle-age in order for any true self-reflection to commence.

I had read that Robin Williams once said: "You're only given a little spark of madness. And if you lose that, you're nothing."

I wondered about the people for whom madness was more of a forest fire, consuming everything in its path.

Maybe I was one of them.

Most mad people usually think themselves sane, anyway: you rarely hear a mentally ill person warn people of their predicament as they're usually screaming their latest theory about aliens at the top of their voice.

The irony was they were preaching to the choir in teaching of interstellar life forms for I had long ago decided we could not be alone in the midst of infinity. I found that believing in everything was an easy task, but standing for something was so much harder.

I had not got that far yet, lost as I was in a maelstrom of information after monitoring the insanity in myself and the wider world for most of my adult life. As soon as psychosis and mania had been defined for me I saw their symptoms everywhere: in my parents, government and even myself.

It was most scary when madness was mixed with acute perception. This was a potentially lethal cocktail: if you really opened your heart and perceived all the suffering going on every day you probably wouldn't want to be here anymore either.

The acute perception can also generate or inform the madness. We really DO live in a society in which ALL of the diagnosable mental afflictions and disorders can be easily evidenced. Yet all the while the society itself was powered and directed predominantly by the mad-who-think-themselves-sane.

Thus the escapism intermingled with self-destruction which people such as myself exhibited. Drugs made me feel as though I was enjoying life, even while in truth they were dragging me under.

Chapter Nineteen

"It must be time now that we wrote the REAL history of America," I wrote in my diary one summer's day whilst avoiding the burning intensity of the Sun. Here was my theory:

A bunch of seriously racist, ambitious white folks went looking for gold and found a pot of it bigger than they could have ever imagined. The price of the abundance of natural resources was paid for by the blood of millions of native peoples and animals.

The establishment of America was basically a slow form of rape, a destruction of previous relative harmony. The Native Americans had originally called their land Turtle Island, but America's formative years were akin to a cancer for this place; within a few hundred years the land which belonged to the Native Americans had been reduced to a mere handful of depleted reservations.

The vicious wave of foreign inhabitants which had crashed upon the shores of the Americas now looked outward and wanted to colonise the whole world with its cultures, values and version of history which excuses and mythologises the trajectory of the white man.

Their beloved white Jesus was their main idol, but He would no doubt be horrified by the attitudes and behaviours of some of His most devout followers.

What they want is unclear. Where American imperialism will end is unknown. Currently they

*seem to be eating themselves, but during the
1960s there was a real push for a new way of
living. When the brave leaders of these cultural
changes were mostly assassinated the whole
movement lost momentum.*

*Since then a kind of tangible depression has
sunk in, a resignation to evil forces, a surrender to
the status quo, an apathy in the face of outright
physical, mental and spiritual warfare.*

Even these descriptive words, let alone the reality
of the events, made me want to scream. This was
the feeling I couldn't put to paper, this was the cry
which simultaneously hid behind my every word.

I was trying to figure things out in my own way
and in my own time - who could blame me? It was
quite the puzzle! The best minds went mad trying to
find the truth of life; the worst minds were too lazy
to try.

It was my strongly held belief that there was a
truth of life, but that a billion agile minds could not
begin to fathom the totality of it. If we pooled our
individual wisdom perhaps we could get
somewhere together, but so many approached the
table with counterfeit notes or poorly scrawled
impersonations of intellectual currency that the
whole process of evolution became ever more
chaotic.

Yet the thing about a life filled with trials and
tribulations was that it was also notoriously full of
spiritual riches. So it was for me as I found myself
a circus freak of ideas, drowning in an

accumulation of perceptions gathered from sources near and far.

Indeed my own wisdom scared me and others, pitiful though my collection of insights may have been in the objective scheme of things.

It was the same situation with all of my friends: each dear soul had some sort of ethereal magic to them, something entirely aside from the ordinary: extraordinary beings walked this Earth and I was lucky enough to really know a few for a short period of time. We may have tolerated each other at worst, but at our dazzling best every one of us celebrated the existences of the others.

It seemed bizarre to me, when looking at the wider world, how so much information translated into so little collective wisdom: we knew how much the icebergs were melting, yet we did less than nothing about it and we'd soon know everything about everyone, yet we were incapable of all getting along. Shocking statistics were met with a chilling apathy by the general public and apocalypse fatigue would soon be considered a thing, I was sure of it.

It was the palpable indifference of the populace coupled with the distress of a few perceptive people which worried me the most. The idea of being 'woke' was bandied about in a Monty Python manner: "Are we or are we not awake?"

The irony was those in power tangibly enforced a comatose state on the public they claimed to serve and openly waged war on social consciousness. Ministers would speak out against the poor and

defend the rich: "For the few, not the many"
seemed to be the unspoken governmental motto.

Meanwhile I languished at the very bottom of
the class hierarchy with plenty of company: the
forgotten people living neglected lives, listening to
Radiohead to get them through.

"How cheap the lives of the poor are," Johnny
had mumbled to himself as he read the newspaper
one morning in the summer of 2016.

I honed in on these words as if overhearing a
secret. There was clearly a hierarchical nature to the
value placed on every life; not every Tom, Dick and
Harry had a state funeral and documentaries about
their lives on important anniversaries after they
died. That's before you even begin with the
importance or lack thereof projected onto the rest of
the natural world. Is a blade of grass more
important than a tiger? Was a pride of lions as
important as a white male human? Who decided?

People all over the world struggled with the
narratives of their own stories let alone the wider
scene. Although some people were clearly enjoying
this humanity-commits-suicide film, I wondered if
it wasn't time for a plot twist: the distinct whiff of
revolution was in the air and if I wasn't able to
somehow start it, I was damn well ready to join it.

I began thinking about that time some friends at
primary school joined me in trying to organise a
mass walkout, but no one was brave enough to do it
except me and, with nowhere else to go, I ran home
so fast that I gave myself heatstroke. The next thing
I knew, the police were in my bedroom with the

headmistress and my poor Dad.

"Not cool, Clara, not cool," was all my father could say while forlornly shaking his head in order to try to clear it of confusion. That was my first attempt to really ignite social change.

The second time I really gave it some welly: an acid tab, some c and 3 spliffs down I walked in front of the Mill Road traffic and declared a revolution. But no one would listen to me and they just tried to hurry around the scene I was making.

As a form of insistence I then took my top off, revealing a skinny frame that brought Johnny some concern. When the commotion started instead of the revolution I had desired, I suddenly realised what I had to do and started shouting "Shalom!", the Hebrew word for peace, repeatedly at volume. This seemed to really calm things down.

I moved backwards away from the baying mob that had surrounded me. Back and back I went until I hit something firm, something immovable. It was the door to my local church, St. Barnabas. By now completely tripping and in desperate need of a bassline I instead had to face the emergency services.

Hysterically worried that I would be taken to Fulbourn psychiatric hospital, I babbled like a brook in the back of the ambulance about my family line and all the people of importance I thought myself connected to.

It seemed to work and I soon found myself taken to Addenbrooke's Hospital instead. I was sitting in a daze in the waiting room, tripping balls, when someone asked for my name and what belongings I had on me. Still shirtless, I managed to hold up a handful of keys and simply say "Shalom!"

When I was seen to, I had a huge, arcing trip about Heaven and how close I was to it. The impression of the church door I had backed into was still lingering and whenever I turned around there seemed to be a glowing light or a corridor presumably leading to God; visions which I alone perceived.

I'd had a similar trip in King's Cross as I waited for a train back from a party. The architecture of the station seemed akin to the glass windows of a church; an entrance or glimpse of another world, perhaps.

No doubt there were other worlds, better worlds. That feeling was with me as the nurses at Addenbrooke's attempted to get this shirtless monster to drink some water. Eventually I had slept, awoken and eaten an omelette before being released. I remembered being warned I had almost been sent to psychiatric hospital, but the rest of it stayed in my mind for years as fractions of a whole.

Still, despite my best efforts, there was no real revolution to be found, just the slow demonic march of moral decay.

Chapter Twenty

Even on a good day I was only ever one disaster away from not being able to cope anymore. However, I perceived myself to be stronger than I really was. The weaknesses in my character had already been in turns brutally and cruelly exposed through my relations with others through the years; friends mocked my propensity for madness and lovers had made their desire for others crystal clear.

It remained the case that I merely wanted to love and be loved. Why was that so hard? Almost every man I had found worth loving had flat out refused to reciprocate my emotions, yet even when such wild things as desires synchronised everything else soon fell apart.

It was all I could do not to become homosexual, though I knew it was as unnatural for me to desire women as it was for lesbians to desire men. We're all aliens to someone, I considered, and went on with my day.

Despite my violent objections to organised religion there was something there, some shining truth, that just had to be found. As opposed to a safe haven, religion seemed to be a particularly pernicious version of Chinese Whispers. And yet I continued to find myself to be somewhat of a believer. Maybe I was a deist, someone who did not believe in the revelations of others and instead observed the divine in all things.

Whenever I tried to share my spiritual beliefs there was usually conflict. "Does nobody think of

God anymore?" I asked myself on occasion. Yet everything I saw pointed to a creator in my eyes: in admiring a sunset, a picture of my mother as a child, or literature which tangibly soothed my frustrated soul I found a warm, fuzzy feeling that informed me I was not alone. It could not be denied, though, that with my blur of deism, theism and confusion, I somewhat envied atheists.

"What do you believe in?"

"Nothing."

"What evidence do you cite by way of reasoning?"

"Everything: the wars, the hatred, the seeming lack of divine presence in my life..."

But, I would ask myself, couldn't these great minds find God's fingerprints on all there is? Even a single hair on their head had more ingenuity in its design than any randomness could explain.

God reminded me of His, Her or Its presence in all things, from the smallest detail of a supposedly meaningless life to the polite arrangements of the heavenly bodies, each having the time and space to burn and circle above us, rendering the night sky a stunning canvas.

Whether the artist proved to be divine or merely a series of fortuitous coincidences was in the mind of the beholder, I surmised, and there were as many perspectives as there were life forms.

Even - sometimes thanks to - being totally inebriated, I still found I could feel the divine in my deepest soul. Everyone and everything was holy to me. After all, Patti Smith said so and I agreed:

rather than perceive religion itself as man-made I preferred to think of it as all divine, from the Tibetan Book Of The Dead to the New Testament, but I found this collection of human wisdom to be contradictory and convoluted in parts.

People were altogether ridiculous in so many ways; humanity seemed nothing but a lengthy comedic sketch, but I tried my best not to laugh too much in the face of all the serious man-made problems.

No matter how cold the world would get I simply refused to mirror it. Mine was a heart as warm as a summer afternoon, a loving torch shining optimistically in a dark and hopeless night; I had no intention to let the cracks stop the light from streaming out: shattered rays were better than darkness. I wrote a list in my diary in order to clarify the situation.

Things we can't agree upon:

- Global warming
- Equal rights for all
- Whether to capitalism ourselves to death or not
- Homophobia is wrong
- Transphobia is wrong
- Guns should be restricted/banned
- Religion
- What happens when we die.

I didn't know how to solve even one of these issues, but I realised the problems were adding up.

While the prospect of 80 happy years for a child seemed a delusion in the minds of the mad I could not in good conscience reproduce. Indeed, I was a passionate anti-natalist and wore my heart on my sleeve. I rejoiced with the new arrivals for my family and friends, but remained steadfast in my own reproductive decisions.

Still, I endeavoured to at least interact with the opposite sex. I got chatting to a wild child online, Stefan, and he said it was a shame I didn't live locally to him or I would find out just how wild he was.

"Am I to be denied this fountain of knowledge?" I was aghast at the thought.

After some cryptic declarations as to the force of his wildness I felt I had to be honest: "I'm a bit of a wild child myself, so I don't know who should be warning who."

Nothing came of it: nothing leads to more nothing and something leads to nothing sooner or later. I thought that was what Leo said when he had explained how everything would be meaningless one day, but I was still pondering it.

The truth, should there even be such a thing, was clearly far more nuanced than Leo had calculated in my eyes. It seemed as though everything was simultaneously eternal and ephemeral: those who'd been loved and lost would surely go on in different forms yet the happiest moments of your life slipped through your fingers as sand.

Could anything lead to anything? What was the point of getting up in the morning, if not? No, ideas such as that were a one-way ticket to depression. Couldn't everything equally be meaningful; each feeling leading to others, every moment strung together as beads on a necklace with the highest and lowest points always intertwined? After all, the lows inform the highs and vice versa.

There must be such a thing as achievement, I concluded, and overruled Leo's theory as though it was a loser's philosophy. I didn't appreciate the word "loser" as it implied a hierarchy of success which I was presumably at the bottom of.

Nevertheless, the theft of as little as £70 could sway a person's status from friend to arch enemy and now everywhere I went I worried about seeing people such as Leo despite my position of moral superiority.

Yet another hierarchy came to mind and I thought of the invisible league tables of the inner world. I wondered who were the most giving, compassionate and wise people currently living rather than the richest, vainest or most academically decorated?

It was all so wrong and the seemingly ever increasing materialism and superficiality of the secular world were parts of that. I decided to go out for the night and have a stranger yell cheesy chat up lines in my ear rather than stay at home pondering the planetary ills.

I came back to Johnny's alone in the early hours and considered what was yet to come. I decided that in the future my number one dream invention would be a search engine for the mind and my first question would be: "How many times have I been to Glastonbury Festival?" It would then develop a whole collection of graphs telling me the total number of days I had spent on site, performers I'd seen and who I'd memorably met.

For now I was stuck with the uselessness of the human memory, though I cherished every recallable snippet of experience. I had attended five Glastos at least: 1989, 1991(ish?), 2004, 2013 and 2015.

That was enough to see the changes throughout the years as it grew to bursting with popularity. I had worked a couple of years with the good crew on site, people who cared and whose hearts were breaking at the destruction of the planet; those wise souls who knew something was going very wrong in society, that there was a sickness in the heart of the mainstream but the alternative still had a pulse.

Several times I had cried with happiness while on strolls through the sloping landscape as I found either views or people to stir my spirit.

This startling landscape surrounding the village of Pilton, a few miles from Glastonbury Town, was where I felt that I had truly found my tribe. It was my dream to read poems in the spoken word area one day, but every year I applied and received no reply.

I remembered distinctly when Johnny and I had persuaded one another to venture down there together. 2013 was the year for it, we decided, and drove past Stonehenge to the hallowed fields of Worthy Farm. After Johnny's favourite peanut butter and banana sandwiches and five hours of waiting at the front we watched adoringly as The Rolling Stones lit up the night and temporarily blew the cobwebs of disappointment and dejection in my being to smithereens.

I had so many beautiful memories from my time at one of the biggest and best parties in the world – but not so many memories as lost memories. I remembered taking 2CI and watching the mud beneath my feet warp into volcanos erupting everywhere the raindrops fell.

As a result of my intoxication I turned up to see the band Love a day late, realising something was very wrong when I observed the lack of anything remotely resembling a crowd.

I did, however, make it to Amy Winehouse, The Libertines, Oasis, Bjork, Florence and the Machine and many other memorable acts. The tears of happiness had flowed during Noel Gallagher's guitar solo for Live Forever, an inexplicable moment of delight that was matched only by seeing Radiohead play Nude in New York's All Points West festival in 2008.

One balmy evening back in Somerset I also watched as a sweat lodge ceremony concluded and a handful of naked people formed a circle, dancing and visibly free. As they swayed and sang I couldn't help but realise that human bodies were all the same with slightly different sizes to each feature. My epiphany was that it was amazing how much focus we tend to put on our physical selves when freedom from the tangible chains that bind us was what was really sought.

In my younger days I would make dream catchers in the Kidz Field and ride the beached boats with their ropes to sway them side to side. The beauty of the place was that you rarely met aggressive people or brutes and almost everyone was sound as a pound in terms of their intentions.

If I could only participate in an eternal sun-drenched Glastonbury Festival I would certainly be happy, but sadly this was not even remotely within the realms of possibility and the traumas of the outside world were always a disappointment to return to.

Chapter Twenty-One

Once we had returned to Cambridge after our Glastonbury adventure I was once again confronted with the damaged and joyless psyche of the average person. Opinions and conversations would grate along with my inability to speak my mind with full force in moments of confrontation lest doing so incite retribution.

I remember finding myself embroiled in distressing discussions with increasing frequency, often featuring themes such as sexual assault. I, along with a large percentage of the women I knew, had been the victim of sexual violence, yet I so often found men defending rape as natural, showing sympathy for rapists and mocking victims.

"Karma will eat you alive," I thought as I watched them perpetuate evil, yet I rarely found the courage to return the vitriol that spewed forth from their beings as, for better or worse, it was not in my nature.

Some women I encountered viewed feminism as bad, even when defined as equality, probably because they had been conditioned since birth to accept their position as the inferior gender. Feminists such as myself therefore seemed to antagonize as we illuminated the cages; sadly, many women had long ago decided that they would rather be comfortably imprisoned than free.

Years later, I continued to experience the highs and lows of human existence with Johnny by my side. One afternoon, I again confided in my loyal friend as the turbulence of 2016 drew to an end, just as the sun poured through the window in the front room in its full autumnal splendour, rays forcing their way into our sacred space amidst the plants and artistic debris which dominated the flat.

"I don't know about you, Johnny, but I've given up. It's as though as a species we've drunk the cyanide and are now waiting for the end which will surely come soon."

Johnny found this quite tragic and reassured me with platitudes and compliments aplenty, but somewhere deep down he felt a residing sense of empathy.

He spoke about critical mass and the logistics of revolution, launched into great speeches about how we must always try to better our souls and planet. But it wasn't enough and I cried myself to sleep that night partly wanting this nightmare to be over and partly knowing that unless we changed course all the goodness, balance and beauty in the world would belong to the past too.

A newfound friend, James, was a shaman who knew exactly what was going on, but didn't want to talk about it: in the darkest of times you can't find the words. He had dreadlocks which almost touched the floor and an even more intricate relationship with Glastonbury Festival than me. I elucidated some of my main concerns to him as we strolled the city's sites of natural beauty:

"Where is the green revolution going to come from? Frankly, humanity has stalled at the first hurdle of agreeing that there's an environmental problem."

"I mean, WHY ON EARTH is it taking so long to switch to renewable energy? I live quite a minimalist lifestyle: no flying, little meat and buying organic/recycled products where possible. I can't minimise things much more and it's still not nearly enough. We need systemic change and we need it now!

"Doesn't any country out there want to take the lead and show the world how it's done? Ban fossil fuels, environment taxes on everything bad, the mass planting of new trees. At the moment it's just a free for all and it has to voluntarily stop or else be forcefully stopped by nature itself."

Upon returning to Johnny's I wrote an Orwellian list of alternative governmental promises:

We promise to sell your future in order to line our own pockets.

We promise not to listen when you call out for necessary changes.

We promise to beat the poor into submission and then buy second houses funded by their taxes.

We promise nothing but lies.

I found that being poor in 21st century Britain was akin to being in a waiting room before death: there was no chance of rising up the ranks as the doors in the corridors of power were all locked and impoverished people were blamed for everything from scrounging off the state at their most vulnerable to overpopulating the planet with babies they couldn't adequately provide for.

The most vicious critics of the poor were the rich with their taxpayer-funded second homes and tax loops exploited for personal gains. If a kid gets caught selling drugs he was likely to get a prison sentence, but work alongside the rich in their malicious games of power and you were the most likely candidate for a knighthood.

It was a wonder how anyone could bring themselves to accept such tainted accolades, but so many were grateful for the acceptance and material gains awarded by the upper classes in Britain.

The masses were left treading water in increasingly dangerous currents; many were drowning as others simply watched from their palaces drenched in gold.

I was mumbling one day to James about judging books by their cover when he interjected with an interesting aside: "Should you judge songs by their covers?"

I thought for a moment and produced an opinion which had been years in the making: "I think judgement can be healthy as it suggests discernment, but too much of it is definitely a bad thing."

That didn't really answer his question, but the day went on. The swans swam in the river, the foxes fed from the garbage and the night turned as black as the future seemed to be.

No matter where I looked or who I was with there usually seemed a painful and distinct lack of goodness in the world. The opposite of giving to charity was giving money to make rich men richer, but that's what many found themselves doing during the great passage of life: feeding into the propaganda of corporations and lining the pockets of their shareholders was the capitalist way, but it wasn't necessarily a process that was harmonious with the wider world.

As usual I felt no need to conform to the norm myself, though my family would insist that I at least attempted to. I repeated to anyone who would listen that should normality be definable I could perhaps acquiesce, but without any such fixed goalposts I would only misdirect my efforts and so thought it best to simply be. It was a shame that the state of simply being was not enough for most; it was too often confused with laziness and a lamentable lack of purpose. However, at the time simply being was the very best that I could offer.

Chapter Twenty-Two

I was mid-way through another rant at Johnny's, sipping tea and inhaling toxins as was my wont:

"Because what they teach in schools is not the reality of life: we are given no skills or knowledge to really tackle the main purpose of our existences, which is to love. On the contrary we are pointed in the wrong direction towards competition and materialism. Maybe in Eastern schools they're teaching things better, I don't know?"

"In what sense?" Johnny interjected after a pause.

"I'm talking about reincarnation, karma and enlightenment. I just feel as though I'm an old soul. Really old. Thousands of years old. I went to an aura-soma reading once and the first thing the woman said to me was that I was an ancient being and that she had images of handprints in the caves of prehistoric France."

"I think I was a dinosaur in a past life," Johnny put forth as tentatively as any deep truth that others would laugh at.

Yet laugh I did - even over Johnny's protestations. And another evening in a troubled world passed peacefully in the flat.

The next day it was my cousin's birthday, so I wished her a happy day and year every day and year, though I knew such a thing was impossible: humans were born screaming and often left the world in a similar state of consciousness; delirious, disorientated and alone. It was all anyone could do to try to bury this fact before it buried you.

Indeed, there was an innate sadness to life that struck me on occasion, sensitive as I was to the general cruelty of existence. Yes, it was a miracle any of us were here at all, but that miracle couldn't dissipate the inherent pain in the process of survival: we watch as the small and great waves of the lives around us crash against the shores of time until finally we ourselves eventually expire.

So I persisted with my wayward behaviour until my cry for redemption became almost audible, my sentences no longer formed correctly and my will to live evaporated as though it was as tangible as liquid, as tangible as love. It was all I could manage to sense this process happening - though, like aging, I could seemingly do little to stop it.

I would no doubt end up lonelier than cat ladies if I wasn't careful, not even a feline friend for company. Speaking of loneliness, one day my mother broke down in tears and said her threshold had been reached. Suicide seemed a most tempting option to her at that point in time and she talked openly of her desire to end it all.

"If you die my only inheritance will be scratch marks on life's door," I said out loud, though it was a poetic statement even for me.

Chapter Twenty-Three

Despite my external problems and disastrous inner world, I continued to reach out to people and nurture connections. I grew increasingly fond of Taylor, finding him to be someone who could lead me astray from my cage. I planned a visit with a couple of friends and made the effort to see him when possible.

You can live like a Queen with a penny in your pocket, I concluded after having spent years in the throes of financial ruin.

"If you can't see the revolution, be the revolution." Taylor instructed in the midst of a downpour in Camden Lock. I thought it akin to a Rumi quote, but couldn't remember which one.

I felt partly blessed and partly cursed as most did, but to an extraordinary degree; it was as if my spectrum of experience was so much broader than the average person. The twirl of a leaf as it tumbled to the floor brought elation and particularly gruesome adverts for charities could make me internally crumble.

Indeed, it bordered on mental illness. One minute I was sitting with God admiring the view and the next the Devil was parading my most private thoughts in front of the whole world; my emotions were a complex series of dominoes which were almost always out of my control.

The best thing to do was to control the stimulus: limit the contact with destructive and self-destructive people, read only peaceful and enlightening literature, avoid all violence and misogyny along with the more distant evils of racism and homophobia.

Being neither a person of colour nor homosexually inclined I could only watch from afar as these wars blazed, cheering on and supporting those who fought for equality and forming coherent answers to the questions posed by bigots.

As a species a frontier was being negotiated in terms of our understandings, lines on the intellectual maps shifting constantly and people battling to claim new territory. But the real casualty on this conceptual battlefield was truth, slayed by the hands of ego and greed. Lies printed daily for all to see, a world seemingly turning too fast.

The battle for wisdom raged on and I couldn't help but be embroiled in it. I thought a great deal on themes such as religion, spirituality and the soul though others called such concepts delusions.

What I found was a certainty that everything happens for a reason, a higher purpose, a karmic debt or reward. But then again, maybe life was a series of flukes and accidents stretching back to the dawn of time as some suggest? When I gazed upon a great natural scene I didn't think so.

In fact my communication with the divine began with numbers when I was a teen. 27 was my favourite number and when I saw it I felt spoken to. The feeling was so wholesome, reassuring and euphoric that seeing 27 anywhere - on my phone, a house or in a newspaper report - became an obsession which consumed my life until I slowly forgot about it. It was perhaps a foray into mental illness, but the lines between madness and sanity would always be notoriously blurry.

It took years for me to realise that I was prone to such obsessive behaviour. Romantically speaking at first there was Daniel, my first love. Then there was Peter, the guitarist in a band who gave me tingles to look at. Then came Adam, the academic who looked himself away like a hermit. Lastly there was Paul, another musician with a good heart. This was besides all the infatuations with celebrities, bands and, of course, drugs.

I had a never-ending loneliness which was only ever temporarily sedated. In reaching out to people, numbers and God I was attempting to find my sense of internal balance, though I walked clumsily on the existential beam.

Everyone struggles to understand this world. To some extent all become lost in a storm of ideas and concepts. People may look sane in a suit or a nice black dress, but really they may as well be wearing straightjackets. For they were participating in a procession of greed, egotism and prejudice amounting to the most insane system of being the world has ever known. I thought on some days that in some ways we were all digging our own graves through buying into the mirage of normalcy.

Nevertheless, there were now around 8 billion people trying and failing miserably to all get along. Some people may also have felt that life was all about watching selfish people find great success, yet in my mind the victories of the immoral were merely temporary. Still, if what didn't kill me would only make me stronger I should have been invincible by now. Why did I at times feel so weak?

Every time I fell, Johnny would pick me back up again: some kind words, a warm smile or something stronger always connected me once again to a deep sense of gratitude I found it hard to word to him.

"Do you know what you are, Clara? You're a wondrous creation," Johnny said on so many occasions. Sometimes he would mix it up and employ the adjectives "wonderful", "amazing" and even "holy" to describe the light within my being that he saw glowing brightly.

Many months passed between these utterances, but by a certain point I became familiar with the game.

"Do you know what you are, Clara?" came to be answered with a flurry of hyperbolic self-praise.

"I'm a supernova burning in slow motion, illuminating everything I touch!" was one such attempt to answer the question. Johnny finally thought he'd talked some sense into me.

Chapter Twenty-Four

Sometimes it's good not to say too much, sometimes it's bad to say too little; learning the difference between the two takes a lifetime.
Unexpressed feelings would in time become inexpressible when repressed for far too long, yet a person with no filter scares the shy and retiring.

Thus went my scrawled, contemplative diary entry for the day. Basically I was learning how to channel my nature through the lens of my conscious mind: learning how much to give of myself and who to pay attention to were art forms I had become determined to master - the consequences for not doing so (or even doing so incorrectly) could be fatal.

When to speak and when not to speak? What to say and what not to say? Who to speak to and who not to speak to? These were all questions requiring some degree of forethought and, eventually, reflection, for it was every soul's work to build an understanding of how to spend the currency of love.

I dwelt intensely on the dreams which were slipping through my fingers. I wanted to be a professional poet, but the infrastructure wasn't there: no one helped me, least of all my family. Also no one believed in me, least of all myself. These were serious internal problems and I could only watch in horror as the fantastical ambitions I fuelled in my own mind slowly morphed into external nightmares.

I wanted to sell a million copies of my book, yet in reality I had sold only a handful. I wanted to be someone great - or at least someone. Instead I was the troubled sort; I found only a frightful nobody when I searched for myself in a mirror.

Gradually the discord between my inner world and outer experiences grew visible, audible and even tangible as my ambitions turned in on themselves. Ideas of who I could one day be gathered as though ghosts which haunted the quickly passing days in an era of my life which was increasingly characterised by chaos. I found that we all had our dreams and delusions, but telling the difference between the two was notoriously difficult.

Yet literature had not abandoned me yet and that evening I read a quote that stunned me: "When the missionaries came to Africa they had The Bible and we had the land. They said 'Let us pray.' We closed our eyes. When we opened them we had The Bible and they had the land."

These words were spoken by Desmond Tutu, yet the specifics of the imagery were soon forgotten, drifting like hazy smoke out of the window of my mind. The next morning Johnny and I were once again shooting the shit.

"I find it ironic that Islam prohibits alcohol, yet it is central to the most important Christian rite," Johnny considered out loud one day as the rain poured outside, limiting everyone's capacity for adventures.

"Interesting observation. Your thoughts are to

your credit," I returned before taking a long, appreciative drag on a peace pipe.

"Also, did you know there's a correlation between the number of churches and the number of strip clubs in cities in the US?"

"Hilarious! Also very telling." I spoke and then, sitting up from a reclined position, passed him the joint as if rewarding the sharing of this information. "Immorality and the need for morality do tend to go hand in hand."

I had actually spent between four and five months Stateside and it was nothing if not eye opening. I went to museums filled with memories of the Boston Tea Party, the founding fathers and the mafia. To my profound dismay, there was but one dusty backroom cupboard for all Native American history.

I had an eating disorder the first time I ventured across the Atlantic as a teenager, skipping meals and running late at night. I came back and my teacher at college felt compelled to check on my mental and physical wellbeing; no one ever checked on the state of your soul, it seemed.

The second time I went Stateside I travelled coast to coast with my future ex-fiance: New York, L.A., Big Sur, San Francisco, Las Vegas were all curious, but my absolute favourite city was found in the far northwest. Seattle had birthed so many of my favourite people that I couldn't help but fall for its considerable charms.

I hadn't been on a plane since then, of course. I felt passionately that flying was a necessity and not a casual pastime. Going to Croatia for the weekend was definitely not my idea of a good time and I quietly frowned upon friends who enjoyed a jet-set lifestyle. Still, I was not the Carbon Footprint Police and so many aspects of life were simply beyond my control.

I only hoped that my care and concern registered somehow. Perhaps in the collective subconscious or somewhere even more obscure, our knowledge of outer reality being just as juvenile as that of our inner worlds.

I had come to believe that the first step on the journey to living our dreams was to feel worthy of achieving them. So, riddled with a disease called hope, I started to submit my poetry to publishers, diligently selecting suitable examples of my work. Waiting eight weeks for a copy-and-paste, impersonal reply - if I even received one at all - was agonising.

I observed that in any vocation there is a thin line between professionalism and malice: Nazis were merely following orders and those who rejected my literary ambitions often swiftly and violently deflated my dreams.

I had collected written proof that some did not read cover letters, let alone my work: in one instance they had even mistitled my book.

It was bad for my mental health, but the publishers cared not for my numerous personal afflictions. Could I make them any money? Probably not. Could I seduce history wholly with my combination of linguistic skill and wisdom? No one seemed to want to read my samples for long enough to find out.

Another day, another way I would find myself misunderstood and degraded.

"I've decided Hell can't be worse than this," I confided in Johnny at long last.

Not knowing the extent of my suffering rendered a suitable reply impossible for the wizened Englishman.

How do you sleep in a world in which terrible things happen to lovely people and lovely things happen to terrible people? It was hard, as I was finding one Winter's night.

I often dwelt upon those who had died for a cause - a long list which Jesus resided at the top of - and concluded that it was better to die for something than live for nothing. I had a habit of doing my spiritual equations out loud with Johnny as my only audience:

"All over the world there are wars in the name of one God or another, but without identifying as a stereotypical Christian, Jew or Muslim I guess I have no cause for which to live and die."

"Isn't love enough?", Johnny enquired with a slow nod in reply.

Belief gave me the hope, courage and bravery to face another day knowing there would one day be no tomorrow, but I was starting to see why people crucified Christ, murdered John Lennon, Martin Luther King Jr., Gandhi and Malcolm X yet allowed men half the stature of these heroes to flourish unimpeded: people were terrible, I concluded, and consequently tried to share as little of my true self with as few people as possible in order to survive the onslaught of abuse, hatred and prejudice I so often encountered.

If it wasn't my gender, it was my class; if it wasn't my drug habits, it was my weight. I seemingly could never win in the sense of being allowed to be truly and wholly myself.

Indeed the masks and duplicitous identities had already been constructed; they formed a cage of deception from which I could no longer escape.

Only when I was alone could I find some respite from external requirements and even then this time was always running out before the next stage show, an ordered farce of shallow lines and truth avoidance. It was all I could do to breathe in and out without the imposition of someone else's rules of how to properly do so.

In other parts of the world many women were not so lucky: they no longer inspired or expired on mad trips around the Sun. Their physical selves had been rendered null and void due to the nature of what was between their legs and the supposed implications for their hearts, minds and even souls.

Sad little men spent their days miscalculating everything and then pinning little bits of stolen gold onto one another's bloody uniforms to celebrate. History books were strewn with brutes and murderers, paraded as the best of us when in fact they were the worst. Survival of the fittest was now survival of the richest - the poor presented no clear worth at all.

Thus I found myself, lying alone and staring at the blackened ceiling hoping for signs of redemption and finding only the darkness of the recesses of my own mind externalised in the disordered shadows.

Nothing seemed right, nothing good; it was a blessing of sorts because the right and good don't last long in this world.

There had been some whispers of a new insult: woke, which I declared I proudly was! I was awake and alive, conscious in a world of economic zombies and refusing to donate my existence to The Man. After all, was The Man Satan himself? Sometimes it seemed so.

In other words I was a layabout. A druggy. A crusty. A hippy. A commoner. A slut. A drain on the economy. A criminal. An outsider. A waste of oxygen in the eyes of the rich. And, at times, I was even a thief, though I only stole from supermarkets when I was really broke and hungry.

Still, at least I wasn't a fun sponge.

Chapter Twenty-Five

While navigating mazes of fate and karma, I stumbled about the world as if blindfolded by its cruelty: I could no longer see the love which was omnipresent in each moment or the victory of survival itself. The yin and yang, the light and dark, the ups and downs left me dizzy with despair.

The stupidity of the average person had become almost tangible, a quicksand of ignorance and ill-informed decisions. Even leaders who carved placating, well-meaning sentences about progress were emotionally illiterate, knowing virtually nothing of the suffering they oversaw.

Competent leaders would find solutions to the problems the world faced, but because global leaders were almost unanimously incompetent they could only find excuses.

The greenhouse gases continued to be emitted, refugees continued to drown in perilous oceans and war wreaked havoc with people's collective and individual well-beings. It was a wonder anyone could prevail in such an environment.

Indeed I felt myself to be slipping under: waves of elation and depression crashed against the shores of my soul in equal measure, my dreams of stability dashed against the rocks of time.

I was confronted daily with the powerlessness of the individual in the face of systemic failure. I sensed the world was heading towards oblivion and I had the map with an alternative course in my hands, but no one listened to the young. The older generations - the metaphorical drivers – generally preferred to increase speed with no real sense of direction as they had been taught by those who came before them.

The trouble was this social system no longer worked and so no one knew what to do anymore. The solutions required thought, planning and, yes, change. Some weren't prepared to admit any fault and spent their time gaslighting the entire world by feigning that life was going smoothly for the majority of its inhabitants.

Of course, it wasn't - even I knew that much. When I engaged with the mainstream media and politicians all I digested was a steady diet of lies, lies and more lies. It was a wonder there were any sane and reasonable folks left among us for I feared they were a dying breed.

"Darker than dark is a Tory heart," Johnny spat on occasion.

It was difficult to decipher what kind of hellish literary visions tomorrow would conjure, but mostly reality seemed a toss-up between a Dickensian or Orwellian dystopia

Although I considered all beings holy, some clearly failed to realise this. That's why I was a passionate vegetarian who avoided all meat whenever possible. The exception to this dietary regime was the Christmas period as I didn't want to make such a fuss that a nut roast was required.

In the chilly build up to the festive season I bumped into a strange-looking woman while strolling clumsily down Mill Road. The creature had all the hallmarks of a beggar, with a spindly frame riddled with desperation, a soul in a state of abject despair.

It was another of those occasions where I wasn't fit for engagements with the general public, but the stranger wouldn't let me pass without incident.

"You! I have summat to tell you," the peculiar figure dribbled, a beer in her hand and a vicious light burning brightly in her eyes.

"Be the reason someone believes in God..." a pause erupted as the stranger struggled to regain her balance. "...and aaaangels," she enunciated with emphasis, elongating the word as though casting a spell. "Rather that than be a servant of the emptiness of atheism!"

She squealed, prowling now and casting her gaze around the scene, an inebriated intellectual boxer spoiling for a fight. Finding no other audience besides my startled self, the withered frame leaned in close and with beery breath finished her message: "Those who look around, see all this beauty but do not recognise its source are blind, while those who claim life is purely hardship should merely look a little closer."

I was about to share my own stuttering belief in the divine, but with that the troubled figure surrendered to old age and parked herself on a nearby bench to continue pouring alcohol down her throat with ease. I decided the woman must be mad, thanked her for her words and wished her well in a glib fashion before continuing to walk into the sunset, baffled by these developments in an increasingly weird world.

Upon returning to my family home I was greeted by all of the conversations I wished I'd never had in one single barrage of hatred. As a result I proceeded to hibernate in my childhood bedroom. Being a staunch atheist, my mother preferred to focus on what she quaintly termed 'reality': no job, no money and no home of my own meant bleak predictions for the future from my supposed closest ally.

Being so spiritually dislocated, I considered us to be talking different languages with the same tongue: the only time I ever heard my Mum hint at any belief in a God was when she said "No one knows what I've been through, only me and my maker."

Aside from that, any mention of divinity was met with a stone wall of silence past which I dared not venture, for I already knew what would happen if I expressed too much honesty.

On one occasion in the distant past I had managed to ignite a fierce debate about basic faith and Mum said "Why do you believe in God? You think someone designed THIS?" She gestured broadly around her ample frame, illuminating the way in which in every corner chaos and cobwebs seemed to be forever intermingling.

I felt dispirited by most conversations, but particularly those with my overtly tormented mother. However, I had decided long ago that I was surrounded predominantly by the jibber-jabber of broken minds and paid my struggling matriarch's valid points little mind.

Instead my diary was reached for as though the written word was my only source of spiritual nourishment: I had a quite desperate need to collate some of my own scattered thoughts, these shattered shards of broken glass that all too often cut deeply to contemplate.

Self-doubt steals dreams, which burst like bubbles at the touch of insecurity. Too much shyness and hopes soon become poisonous; the suppressed inner world akin to a Munch painting, whirling and disturbed by ambitions beyond the reach of self-belief.

I then spent the night playing guitar and wrote a song to encapsulate it all.

In The Arms Of The Universe

I'm finding a need to be alone with myself,
I'm finding it hard to be around anybody else.
You wouldn't believe what's on the news today;
If these people had consciences they would feel shame.

Yesterdays haunt my mind
Every time I close my eyes.
These visions of love
Will conquer me,
So wrap your arms around me
Until I can't breathe.

I'm in your arms.
I'm in your arms.

But it's not up to you
What I do with my body.
It's not up to you!
It's not up to anyone but me.

It's not up to me
To help you look beyond your nose.
Oh, you're so blind
Everybody knows.

If you believe in a good God
To help us through
When times get hard,
Your great guide
Must know me too
And there must be something that we can do?

I'm in the arms of the universe.

Upon putting aside my cheap Spanish acoustic
guitar, I was satisfied that I had sung from my very
soul. I then wrote scattered thoughts in my diary
once again, this time regarding the state of the
music industry:

No one writes songs with meaning anymore
because they're cluck cluck CHICKEN!! I've got
something to say - shoot me then! Destroy all

*meaning wherever it's found and leave the world
lonelier than the Sun, burning in the night until the
morning comes. Sleeping babes within the shade lie
scattered as petals on a grave. Who died? Who
knows? We're all ultimately strangers to ourselves
and others - the trick is never to be a slave.*

Although I had attempted to write with purpose and
passion it made little sense in truth; I acknowledged
that any real inkling of meaning had dissipated
given the limitations of my talents.

I had then continued with my fleeting attempts
to connect and spent the following evening with
Tom, who for a short passage of time was a
handsome young man-who-would-later-become-a-
woman with whom I shared tabs of acid and I love
yous.

Tom told her a horror story about a friend of his
whose one night stand turned out in the morning to
be a UKIP supporter so far to the right of the
political spectrum as to be declared lost. Whether
the individual in question was merely morally
unhinged or an incarnate existential faux pas was a
matter of compassion, of course, but Tom and I
found the concept of such a sly misguided lover
laughable nonetheless.

As for me, I had only once slept with a Tory and
wouldn't repeat the experience. I didn't find out
about his fascist leanings until after the act and then
swore never to go back; it was a promise I had kept
without effort.

However, I did have dear friends who voted for

the Conservatives. They were often visibly confused about why and occasionally they would defend the indefensible with the lives they patently deemed worthless.

I tactfully avoided all political discussions in these relationships, but when I was forced by such company to have dreaded political encounters they would too often be littered with stark, outrageous ignorance. When I bravely asked for an opinion on the leader of the opposition, for example, I was met with blank faces and worrying questions.

"Who's that?" came one such response.

I sensed a portion of inner wisdom break the surface of my mind: "No need to mock a person who makes a mockery of themselves. That's the cousin of bullying!"

The doors of perception bent like spoons the following evening as I was gently ushered by haunting voices down a great hallway of understanding. I beheld global problems and famous faces blurring, all specific meanings redundant; I felt a sense of elation mingle with sheer terror while unclear which emotion was the more powerful: there was a thin line between living a dying, I surmised.

I sail to the East
Of my consciousness.
See things I'd never seen,
The truth of my unhappiness.
Nooses of sex,
Chess boards of desire.

I play then get strung up.

So I sail to the West
Of my consciousness,
Learn things I'd never guess
In newfound happiness.

Conscious, can't move,
My mind's blouse undone.
What truth is here!

I wine and dine our unendingness
Until I can't breathe for contemplating breath.
Quickly, touch me without the use of skin!
And I'll recover
To watch poets make a muse of time
As if they're courting it
And then die just like illiterates.
Tender lover, not of flesh and bone,
Please don't hurt me like them.

This trip wasn't entirely pleasant and the time spent alone was the worst. Images of blackened teeth chattering appeared in the dusty window and the state between life and death seemed to be the focus of my conscious attention. Visions of the nature of the afterlife were never the most calming, lacking as they did an appreciation for the living.

It was not an experience bereft of deeper insights, however: glimpses of my mortality with only the company of an elderly man to call upon as a distraction was not ideal, but the universe was

trying to say something about the close proximity
of death that I would ponder for years afterwards.

Once I had made it through the jungle of this
sensory overload I then proceeded with the
drudgery of a relatively sober mind. Upon writing,
however, I found the right words wouldn't come
easily.

Love

It's in the air,
So breathe it in -
This love thing,
It's no sin.

It's in your food
And in your drink;
All these gifts
Must make you think?

It's in the night,
All through the day;
Don't let hate
Get in the way.

Love on!
Because it feels good
To do right
As you should.

I decided that what I had written was a terrible
attempt to honour the sense of omnipresent love

which had on occasion overwhelmed me: I screwed up the piece of paper I had scrawled my seemingly worthless rhymes on and threw it into the corner of Johnny's spare room.

It was later to be found by Johnny, who savoured every word. It had caught his attention during a rare cleaning session and profoundly touched his weary heart.

The wizened gentleman must have felt that to know the dreamer who wrote these stanzas was a gift beyond measure and, although I had trouble knowing it myself, this scrawled poetic offering further reinforced his perception of the goodness in my deepest soul. Johnny put the crumpled sheet in his diary, but never told me of his discovery. I was to find it years later in more sombre circumstances.

Chapter Twenty-Six

I went round a friend's and had another philosophical discourse that I soon forgot the details of, but which had seemed important at the time. I then walked back to Johnny's and had a light session in order to reach the conclusion that philosophy was amazing - except for the misogyny.

Between us we competed to see who could find the most sexist quote by an esteemed thinker. There were many options. Socrates said women should have the same pursuits and activities as men, "but in all of them woman is inferior to man." Schopenhauer suggested that "a woman needs a master." Aristotle declared that "...the male is by nature fitter for command than the female." Rousseau thought that "the education of women should always be relative to that of men. To please, to be useful..." Kant believed that "a woman is little embarrassed that she does not possess high insights; she is beautiful...that is enough..." Nietzsche went further and stated that "one-half of mankind is weak, chronically sick..."

With every misguided sexist sentiment Jules, who had encamped in the flat for several days now as a result of his homelessness and general lack of support, voiced a roar of approval. Despite my sympathy for his unstable circumstances, I did not take kindly to his attempts at humour:

"Are you fucking thick or just wilfully ignorant? Why am I worth less because I'm a woman? You're worthless because you're a fucking dickhead!"

At this Jules retreated from the debate, preferring to smoke for solace in the corner of the room, resigned as he was to the peripherals of the conversation from that point on.

He piped up only once again in the conversation to say that his anarchist friends believed people who read religious and spiritual books have "woolly minds."

This again offended me in a primal, visceral sense. The viciousness of my own words then took me aback.

"I'd rather have a woolly mind than a closed mind," I spat in his general direction while reaching for the joint in order to cope with such ignorance.

If minorities such as gays and transgender folk were slandered in such a manner it would rightly elicit uproar, yet believers in anything had become fair game in terms of mockery and open derision.

This seemed to be the attitude of the day: "I don't believe in anything and if you do it is laughable; you are an intellectual invalid talking to an imaginary friend in your deepest prayers, nothing more."

I found all of this objectionable and more than a little akin to a lazy man's solution to a particularly arduous inner journey: simply don't begin.

As opposed to my distaste for Jules and his obnoxious presence, I had many questions for Johnny: "Why's misogyny so normalised while feminism's seen as radical? I've known people who'd never heard of misandry before because it's so rare. Yet hatred of women is ingrained in human history, growing around the world partly in response to the minor hard-won victories claimed by so-called feminazis," I expanded upon the earlier points, furious as I was in a pure, spiritual sense.

"Injustice anywhere is a threat to justice everywhere," as Martin Luther King Jr. had once said. I believed it with my whole heart.

"The future of humanity, if there is to be one, most certainly belongs to women. A feminist, to me, is merely someone who believes in equality. If fighting for equal rights for all is radical that's a sad indictment of our current state of affairs," Johnny thoughtfully replied.

Some raged against the dying of the light as Dylan Thomas had advised, but others seemed to rage against the illumination of the dark. Strange as it may seem total equality was indeed frowned upon by those with a vested interest in maintaining historical hierarchies.

Unlike Jules, Johnny recognised the truth in my thoughts and words and supported me every step of the way as I attempted to grow into a woman with a sure sense of her own subjective definitions of right and wrong.

No matter where one stood on the great spectrum of opinions it could not be denied that, even objectively speaking, women had historically been pushed out of mainstream discussions, rejected in their findings and neglected in terms of their potential.

A quote by Mary Wollstonecraft came to my whirling, mercurial mind: "Taught from their infancy that beauty is woman's sceptre, the mind shapes itself to the body, and roaming round its gilt cage, only seeks to adorn its prison."

Women were killed by men every day, men were killed by other men every day, but it was doubtful men were killed by women every day despite the provocation.

Females were clearly the fairer sex in my eyes purely because we had never collectively attempted to imprison anyone except arguably ourselves, never used force to impose nonsensical beliefs en masse and scarcely a solitary one of us had been foolish enough to believe the world could be ruled.

On the contrary, females on the whole had accepted their fates as citizens who were degraded in every realm of life with a quiet resignation and gentility which revealed the fallacy of misogynistic ideas: sexism was nothing but a second-hand lie passed down as a faulty heirloom might be from fathers to sons and this evil had now spread so far and wide that even the mothers and daughters at times fell prey to the flawed logic of such theories.

It was sad that women had fought and died so that I could vote between Dickhead A or B. I had come to believe that men in general had forgotten how to defend and protect women, now regularly assaulting and degrading my sex as bullies who could sense the fear in their victims. Predators detect frailty in their prey and perhaps female kindness was, after all, simply a weakness in a notoriously brutal world.

Little did men know that women secretly wanted to be treated as princesses: the males of the species would rather dictate their own degrading definitions of the opposite sex rather than listen to the inner fantasies of the other.

I felt the stage was set for a spectacular woman to come along and show other women how to live, but at the moment many females (myself included) seemed lost; devoid of a feminine Saviour, betrayed by lovers and being constantly othered in this great human march of progress.

All across the world the rights of women and girls were being challenged and eroded. What did men do about it? They responded to polls by saying women's rights had gone "too far". It was enough to make me weep, but there I was dry-eyed and traumatised by the toxicity of the atmosphere in which I found myself.

Growing up in a world which was so deeply patriarchal was distressing to me as with many young women. Those who would not submit to male superiority risked threats, isolation and violence. Women and girls everywhere were forced to decide whether equality was a hill worth dying on and clearly many had reached a negative conclusion.

Finding figures who made a difference in the fight for equality was difficult: many female philosophers, scientists and writers had been written out of the history books on account of their sex regardless of their ingenuity.

Religious figures who happened to be female had even historically been declared prostitutes by the Church, such as the infamous slandering of Mary Magdalene by Pope Gregory the Great in AD 591: the religious institutions which dominated the world were hellbent on ensuring a woman's place remained split between the kitchen and, if married, the bedroom (though her sexual pleasure was to be passionately feared and openly loathed).

Yet I still found strength in Jesus: although Christ was a man, He was not a misogynist let alone a racist or raging homophobe. His holy teachings spoke purely of love, yet Christ's message had been manipulated by mere mortals in order to spread hatred. Love thy neighbour as thyself, the golden rule of Christianity, had no asterisk disqualifying women and gays, though some of His followers may wish that it did.

Still, no matter which gender was preferable to whom, without each other there was nothing. As a result of such conversations I dwelt upon my leg-shaving, eating disorders and hair straighteners; I couldn't for the literal life of me figure out how to escape the confines of femininity other than to forego interaction with most men. I wasn't sure I was ready to do that just yet, but perhaps a relatively monastic existence would be my eventual fate.

I then pondered whether or not I should go and live in the woods as some of my friends had done and completely reject the capitalist system we are all entangled with since birth. However, the overbearing nature of the logistics involved along with the isolation required seemed too much to even contemplate at length let alone put into practice.

After such difficult topics of conversation I was too frightened to sleep. Yes, I was afraid for the females of the future, but it had become the same thing every night: what would tomorrow bring? Where was I going besides oblivion? I had become ambivalent about whether it was a fast or slow process; I just didn't want to suffer anymore.

What was life besides suffering?! Not much, I had come to conclude. Just a glimpse here, a whisper there of a happiness that was impossible to maintain. Only when slightly adrift from reality could I find any real beauty or substance in the world, in life itself.

I felt myself to be utterly alone, as alone as a human could be, while surrounded by those who cared only for themselves.

Obviously there were exceptions to this rule, but they were few and far between: I wasn't sure if it was Thatcher's evildoing or God's supposedly flawless design, but people seemed to care less and less for others.

Even my collection of books horrified me. I'd been forced to throw several aside, riddled as they were with prejudice, torture and confusion which far outstripped my own. Yet if the reviews were to be believed these were some of the finest offerings humanity had to show for itself; it all seemed too little and too much simultaneously.

There was such a scarcity of that which was pure and good, God's touches upon my life were seldom felt - if at all. Most 'normal' people argued that divinity was an enduring delusion, but I once again went looking for truth: I decided to venture beyond the door of the local Church, St. Barnabas, and attend a Sunday service. The polite conversations over tea and biscuits were as far removed from the blood and wailing of the crucifixion as it was possible to be, but still the sacred thread which connects all things held firm.

Everyone was nice, but something was missing: I was clueless about the melodies of the songs, the correct responses to the preachers' sermons or the right way to behave. Should I feign meek piety, I wondered, or would that be a sinful lie?

Some members of the congregation were clearly experiencing something far beyond that which I was at that point capable of. I had even attended services where a few had cried. Presently many waved their hands in the air at pivotal points while I stood soberly observing the scene. Friendly as modern Christians seemed, they were not my tribe.

After all, following my extensive Biblical exegesis I had found myself a non-believer in holy scriptures of all varieties. Misogyny was in every text declared to be God's own that I had ever come across - I was sick of reading the toxic theories of cruel men as if they were in any way revelatory or indicative of a higher power.

In The Bible Timothy exclaimed "I suffer not a woman to teach, nor to usurp authority over the

man, but to be in silence." In the Quran
Muslim men are told "Your wives are your tilth;
go, then, unto your tilth as you may desire". In
Buddhism, the so-called holy books
described the life of Siddhartha Gautama and
suggested that "letting women into a holy place is
like letting a plague of locusts into a field of crops."

I found such analogies less than helpful. Given
such historical attitudes it was hardly surprising that
misogyny was so prevalent in the world despite
notable progress. If females were thought dumb by
intellectuals, objectified by artists, relegated by
politicians, starved by fashionistas and came into
being as an afterthought of the divine, how was I
supposed to love and value myself?

The answer was I could not: all of my learning
only guided me further from self-love and the
heartfelt acceptance of who I was.

It was a wonder I believed in anything at all
given God's apparent hatred of me and my kind.
Why invent females only to belittle us and diminish
our power forevermore?

No, such ideas stained a holy being with the
fingerprints of mortal men. But there must
something - anything - to believe in which was
pure, true and good?

Furthermore I found that, on top of the more
challenging parts of the accepted holy
scriptures, some people deliberately misinterpret
the texts, wilfully so: they used religion as an
excuse to hate, when really it implored you to love.

As with all mere mortals, although my God

didn't make mistakes, I made plenty. Still, I needed faith as a light bulb required electricity, seeking as I was only to shine amidst the darkening night of hopelessness and despair.

It just felt to me as though big-hearted people who cared about the world and others were more likely to get used, derided or even killed rather than celebrated. The world was clearly run by those who didn't care about the environment, the future or others and I was not alone in finding the whole situation horrific. Maybe I was one of those who were too afraid to care lest my soul break as well as my heart.

I was blowing a fuse in slow motion and needed to vent. Upon returning to Johnny's I found a multitude of guests coming and going as I tried hard to formulate my frustration in words:

"I don't know about you lot, but every day is getting more of a drag than the last one. No one better invite me to a house party anytime soon as I will be the grouch in the corner suppressing the urge to shout 'what a load of bollocks' every five minutes. It wouldn't be anything personal, just some kind of abstract existential protest about nothing in particular and ALL OF IT," I mused to the gathering.

"This is all just fucking bollocks. Total and utter bullshit is everywhere I look, even within. Half the time I don't know whether I'm sad or angry, but then again it's the complete emptiness I feel the rest of the time which really scares me."

"Dear one! Not all of us are the problems; some

of us are the solutions," Johnny tenderly proffered.

I was having none of it.

"Sadly we are each of us complicit with this mad destruction of all that is whether we like it or not: by merely breathing we are partaking in this demonic species and its disgusting ways. I am a prisoner in this world in many ways, but I'll still stay and fight for a better future - even if I have to do it alone."

I was never alone with Johnny by my side, though. I felt and appreciated his care for me and although night turned into morning before we could all finally get some rest, we were by that point feeling slightly better having communicated with our hearts as always on our sleeves.

"In a society that convinces people that like attracts like AND opposites attract no wonder we're confused," I spoke out loud to Johnny the next day while pondering my love life over a peace pipe.

The popular musician Ed Sheeran came on the radio and Johnny disagreed with me regarding his musical worth: I groaned and complained that he didn't inspire, but was merely a corporate entity with a hollow centre. "He's a sell-out!"

However, Johnny quite liked him. "You can't sell out if you've got nothing to sell out in the first place," he wryly observed.

I admired Johnny's ability to really go there as most people ran screaming from interactions about anything besides the weather.

"Not many people have seen what you've seen: most people don't even have their eyes open," I

complimented him by way of thanks for
his being.

The conversation then seemed to trail off after
Johnny's gratitude was sincerely expressed, so I
dramatically suggested a new verbal challenge to
toy with.

This time it was personal.

"Johnny what would you change about me?" I
enquired with a burning curiosity.

"You are a bit sweary," Johnny sheepishly
suggested.

"Too fuckin' sweary?!" I said, outraged. "Ah,
shit!"

We laughed away another tortured evening
which globally featured rape, murder, incest,
paedophilia and a hopelessness that temporarily
seemed far away. We may have shared the world
with a motley crew of sexists, homophobes and
racists, but we were very consciously making our
way to the light of eternal, unconditional love.

Chapter Twenty-Seven

I had grown up, but there was one thing that I had forgotten to do: love myself. Loyalty was so rare I could scarcely find it. I had cheated on people and people had cheated on me. The world still went round, but it wasn't supposed to be like this.

When choosing a secondary school my parents had merely gone down the list in the phone book and Coleridge was decided upon. I was swiftly offered drugs aged 12, told my Mum and got pulled out of school.

To get me away from the temptations of modern life my folks then decided to enrol me in the religious school on the street opposite, St. Bede's. The thing was that I had to be christened, so family came from London for the blessed occasion in which I found myself miming the words I couldn't speak.

"Repeat after me," said the priest. "I give my life to the Lord and Saviour Jesus Christ…" But at that age I didn't understand what Jesus would want with my life and refused to verbally accept my position. Thus the ceremony drew to a close and although no one had noticed the inner commotion involved on my part, the violation of my spiritual autonomy had not been entirely unopposed.

In refusing to repeat such words as had been dictated by the priest my relationship with the Lord remained akin to a contract unsigned, a cheque uncashed or an old, unloved virgin: the ultimate transaction had not been completed in my eyes. I would come to believe in my own time and in my own way, but I would not be dictated to.

I went round my newfound school chums' houses to find copies of The Bible strewn around the place, wholly at odds with my own home. However, I settled in well in my new school, even finding myself somewhat afraid of falling behind. I heard several rumours about the nature of the place, primarily that it was one of only a handful of inter-denominational schools in the British Isles and that Bono had come out of the one in Dublin, Ireland. I was sure this was something to be proud of, though other children seemingly felt shame to be associated with such a divisive figure if they felt anything at all.

By all accounts I was a good student who answered well in class and usually did my homework. The only time I got in trouble was during my Food Technology classes when my friend persuaded me first to make battered Mars bars in the practical lesson, then to whip cream and cover the ceiling with it (also smearing some in a pencil case) and finally this behaviour culminated in egging the teacher's house.

When we were called into the Head of Year's office we could barely contain our laughter, but were believed when we had said we didn't do it and dismissed. Outside the room the hysterical roaring commenced, but I also sensed a guilt I felt embarrassed to convey.

Back in the present day, as it was then, I had found another lover. Emmanuel was too handsome for his own good, but I found myself seducing him as if that was a positive thing.

"You think that I think too much of myself, but I think that you think too little of me," Emmanuel said one day after we had made love.

I disagreed, but didn't want an argument so politely laughed. After all, it was laughable. Emmanuel had asked in the midst of the act whether he was the best I had ever had. After two minutes it was too soon to tell and, stunned into silence, I had failed to answer quickly enough.

"I'll take that as a no," Emmanuel decided, though he clearly believed himself to be a living, breathing Adonis.

The worst moment came when he refused to perform oral sex due to my lack of shaving. "You're joking, right?" I uttered in disbelief, contemplating how all those waves of feminism had simply never met his shore.

The next time we spoke Emmanuel requested a repeat experience and I foolishly believed he was seeking to redeem himself. He instead asked me to invite a friend. I was immediately sceptical: not only was I not remotely sexually attracted to females, but I had a bad time with my first threesome with two men in that one was more attractive than the other and both turned out to be assholes – I didn't want to repeat any of those experiences. So I explained how I wasn't a fan of threesomes right before Emmanuel removed himself from my life entirely.

"Well, that went well. What a nice guy," I

thought to myself and then got on with the seemingly infinite pain and unfairness of staying alive.

Next up on the romantic carousel came Ryan. This dashing youth was significantly younger than me, for we had met while he was just a teenager. He was now 21, but only in physical appearance.

We had first encountered one another online and were erotically entwined until Ryan decided one day that he had a new girlfriend. This was fine for me as I had no feelings of love towards myself let alone another.

Then Ryan got back in touch and I paid for a room to invite him to. He travelled from London, where he now lived, said he was tired and after half an hour of foreplay gradually fell asleep. This left me to smoke a cigarette, watch Dirty Dancing and anticipate Round Two.

However, when Ryan awoke he farted loudly before muttering something about "hormone problems", so we simply dressed and left.

I found him altogether repulsive - I spent a sleepless night plagued by inaction before I finally decided to message him in the morning saying I didn't want to see or speak to him again.

Once more the arrogance of my sexual partner overwhelmed any chance of real union, so I chose for a while to embrace the emptiness of solitude which I had come to know so well.

As the years passed, the dating experiences got worse. One time I was even catfished by someone claiming to be a handsome young white man with chiselled abs and pronounced cheek bones. He turned out to be a deceptive pervert who, when I threatened to call the police, replied "You don't like my body?"

Chapter Twenty-Eight

My experiences of love thus far had been as rare as they were true; I remained as a flower seeking the light caress of raindrops yet I dreaded the merciless storms of heartfelt romance.

In my experience, true romance was akin to a natural disaster which stripped everything in its path, flooded even the most guarded heart and left only cruelly misjudged memories and outright despair. Yet despite the acquisition of such hard won truths I continued to keep an open mind.

"You like poetry, don't you?" An attractive gentleman enquired outside the pub that night while we were both ingesting some nicotine.

I was touched that my love of lyrical wordplay layered with similes and metaphors had been noticed by another.

"Everything's poetry, can't you see?"

I threw my arms out and circled in the night sky, luminous just for a moment. Slurring the rhymes with unnecessary emphasis, I then proceeded to vocalise in verse:

"The waves of emotions
Meet the shores of experience
On the great land mass of time,
Which is crumbling even as we speak.
Hope is now but a refuge
For the deluded and the weak.
Come with me, dear butterfly,
Into the warming air we'll glide;

Let's escape the confusion of the known."

I wasn't sure what it meant, but it had felt right to say.

Meanwhile, the young man was slightly startled by the scene which had just played out before him; fantasies had accidentally been surpassed with a perceived grace that would linger within him forevermore. Indeed, he would recall the moment vividly and seemingly at random for many moons to come.

"You might like this then..." He said and handed me a weathered volume of poems I had not yet heard of.

"I hope you love it," he leant into me with a gleam in his eye before this fiercely original being then threatened to retreat to the recesses of my drunken consciousness whereas for a moment he had been front and centre. I baulked at the thought of such a loss and stumbled after him, drunk with my own perceptions as well as through alcohol consumption.

"I'm going to call you Romeo!" I shouted after him, having been made giddy by his presence; after hours of relative reclusion I felt myself to have come to life as a field after rain.

"Why is that?" the handsome stranger called back, seeming mildly perplexed at how forward I was being.

"You look like a Romeo, that's all."

"I wouldn't be so foolish as him," the young man retorted with a glare I could barely make out, but I imagined to be full of self-assurance.

I awoke alone in the morning in Johnny's flat and couldn't shake the feeling that something had happened, something good. The poetry collection lay on the upturned cardboard box which passed as a night stand next to my mattress.

After reading a few verses, I was inspired to write. Yet my words were the thoughts of a maddening mind, equally corrupted by good and evil: my sweetness made me naive, my sadness made me blind. The beauty of life surrounded me, yet I beheld it not: I was lost in a sea of confusion with only my chin remaining above the waterline.

Twin Flames

The wisdom of a thousand lives
You give to me for free;
Love creeping upon me
As a crippling disease.

Infected, malnourished;
I have all but perished.
I'll see you again when I sleep.

You are a living vision to me;
I'm a fantasy to you.
Let's use these God-given imaginations
And dream as lovers do

Of a brighter tomorrow
That beckons and gleams:

Loneliness a thing of the past.

When two souls collide
Deep bruises are felt:
The marks of passion,
Need and strife.

I struggled to pinpoint the exact moment my past had become a ghost, but it began to haunt me. The child I had been, the years now gone, the pictures of my former days: all gathered together to make a ghoul to truly fear.

I was, in fact, running from myself.

Regrets were forcefully repressed while people spread their wis-dumb claiming it's not what you have done that you will most lament on your death bed, but what you didn't do. In my heart I knew it was clearly a balance of both.

The thoughts, words and deeds for which I could never forgive myself regularly knocked at the door of my consciousness. As religious zealots they begged to be let in, given attention and to eventually let their truth be known.

I decided to distract myself from my inner torment and take a trip through town to pick up some food and resources. There were beer boys blaring threats from motorbikes, violins playing gratingly out of tune, street preachers decreeing that "religion kills, Jesus saves" and manic men spewing abstract bile to no one and everyone. The latter scenario featured a madman shouting a stream of garbled insults aimed at the rich and famous who were, in fairness, leading the world off the existential cliff by all accounts.

In short, I found ineffable horror squared as soon as I relinquished the safety of hibernation.

Returning to the flat I now shared with Johnny in a verbally official sense was a relief. My evening would be spent studying what was, namely what was inside the poetry collection the beautiful man at the pub gave me. I wished I could remember his name and felt sure I would see him again. The first poem was bleak.

The Inner Scream

Put on a nice dress
And shave your legs.
There's no need to cry:
Your cell has a soft bed.
Yet the rape, the heartache and the times you've bled
Might make you want to scream.

However, the imagery spoke to me and the meanings stirred. It was written by a technically mad feminist from the States, though I soon forgot her name and couldn't pronounce it anyway. All that remained of my time reading when all was said and done was a feeling that I had been cleansed of falsehood.

Still nothing quite seemed real anymore; not the pressing nature of my sorrow nor the dangers of tomorrow: life was a disturbing dream from which I could not seemingly awake.

Clearly the battle for survival was not purely physical, but was also actively being fought in the mental and spiritual realms. I watched from up close and afar as people fell down, became intellectually twisted or sensed their souls slowly being eked away from within and without.

I had even met those who held my hand tightly while consciously draining me of my already-depleted energetic reserves. It was a wonder I was brave enough to hold anyone's hand, metaphorically or literally, after such experiences.

I just hoped that I didn't join these armies of black hole entities in human form, but one cannot see themselves objectively. The only existential maps I knew of seemed impossible to follow: ultimately I found Jesus too hard to emulate – some even labelled Him unrelatable - and this was evidenced by the way His followers stumbled at every command.

Indeed it seemed to me as though belief in anything at all was being openly questioned in my circles, my wayward devotion to love marking me apart from many of the scoundrels I felt surrounded by.

Attempting any form of achievement seemed overly ambitious, seeing as my survival was seemingly a long shot. I died several times a day; not la petite mort of which the French speak, more akin to a glass shattering.

I was wounded by the insults of men who, upon reading my words, would pick them apart and throw them back at me regurgitated yet bereft of all initial meaning and sense. This killed me quietly, even though I tried not to take it too personally.

The rejections of lovers and friends temporarily stopped my pulse: seeing people I had used to know, but who now deemed themselves too good to talk to me was an experience I sought to reduce the frequency of to no avail.

If anything such incidents became more common as I gazed down the barrel of a gun called Addiction and laughed as a bullet with my name on was loaded. The sheer extent of my misfortune, coupled with my inability to escape from its clutches, was of tragic comedic value.

For strength of spirit and peace of mind I leant upon the words of great writers and poets such as Kahlil Gibran and paraphrased his words to my company for the evening: "The jar which is carved by your sorrow will later contain your joy."

In a very real sense such concepts touched me, spurring me on in my quest for an enlightened state of mind, the Holy Grail of consciousness that seemed virtually impossible to find.

"I don't know how you can remember quotes when I can barely recall my own name," my companion exclaimed once I had paraphrased to him the handful of quotations by Tacitus, Yeats and Rumi that I could easily recall.

"Still, none of us have a clue what's really going on," I assured him. "Some people are able to remember quotations and others less so, but no one really knows what the best life is and how to live it.

I mean, do you know why we're here?"

"Not a clue!" my lover confessed.

"Exactly," I concluded; we laughed and then continued our night of passion after confirming our abject existential confusion. The next morning I busied myself by employing words in order to evoke further meaning in my life.

I'm going to the good side of the sky
When I die,
Where evil cannot go.
But things before then
Of true beauty
I beg of You to show.

Perhaps these ramblings were destined for the overflowing plastic bag I used as a bin at Johnny's place. I couldn't be sure yet. Instead of making an irrevocable decision I ventured out into the night to source some more trouble.

I found myself in the local brew house once again ranting at relative strangers. "I fundamentally believe God can forgive any awful decision, bring back a lost soul from the brink of despair and that this force for good understands me in ways I have yet to know myself."

I wanted to go on, but for a while spoke only internally. "Both dreams and nightmares await us, sometimes twin-born. It is our role in life to find and live God's dreams for us, - the higher calling each of us has which ebbs and flows with different directions and force as with a tide - lest existence become purely a stagnant nightmare."

"Well, yes, but I only remarked upon your crucifix. I think it's pretty," my companion felt a bit taken aback by my barrage of faith.

"It pisses off all the right people," I smiled so hard as I spoke that it rendered my words indecipherable and I had to repeat them with enhanced clarity until, at volume, I was comprehended.

I then seized upon a lull in proceedings once the giggles had subsided, sensing I had something to say.

"I wrote a line last night I thought was really moving," I offered, feeling brave.

"Do I want a line? Why, have you got some coke?"

"No, you idiot! A line of literature, which far exceeds any drugs I can lay my hands on…"

"Oh, really?"

I leant forwards and spoke up: "Unfulfilled potential digs graves, your pity is nothing but flowers laid upon them."

My companion, whose name I could not recall despite us having had several conversations, was less than willing to engage.

"That's nice. Are you doing anything at the weekend?"

I felt unheard once again and sensed my mood immediately plummet. Having provided a piece of my heart on a plate it had subsequently been fed to the proverbial dogs. It was then I decided to verbalise my deepest emotions, which was always accompanied by risk.

"It's not nice, actually. It's very painful to watch people drink, smoke and piss away their lives having disconnected from their dreams long ago."

"Oh, I dare say you're onto something there, lassie! When you put it as you have I can see what you mean."

I was pleased to have fought for and won a sense of connection at long last.

Ray Of Sunlight

I feel like a ray of sunlight
Drifting through some electric blue ocean-like sky.
I'm so extraordinary
Like everything.

You look like a ray of sunlight
Drifting through the electric blue, mysterious ocean
of a sky.
Feel it,
Feel it.
Feel as extraordinary as you are.

Chapter Twenty-Nine

Despite my capacity to write optimistic lyrics, doing so was a futile attempt to remind myself of my own beauty. In reality I was in so much abstract pain that I didn't even cry anymore. After all, what was the point? It would only be misconstrued as weakness.

"I'm in love with madness," I confessed the next day during the course of yet another successful session with Johnny as he called me "milady" and poured another stiff drink.

My hair had been soaked by the rain and he thought I looked lovely as I dried it. He said so several times, though any genuine attractiveness I possessed had escaped full acknowledgement in all my philosophising.

In the process of our conversation, fuelled by the usual medicines, we devised a new word as Shakespeare would in days of old: "feelisation". It was defined as not merely intellectually knowing something, but emotionally understanding it.

This reminded me of Camus' point in 'The Myth of Sisyphus': "These are facts the heart can feel; yet they call for careful study before they become clear to the intellect."

Not to disagree with a great, but in some ways I felt the opposite was true: what is known by the mind takes time to be perceived by the feelings of the heart. For example, you can know that love drives you mad, would see it in your parents and your friends. But you don't fully realise it until you experience such madness yourself. At this point you will have a feelisation about the depth of human love – and insanity.

So it was with me and the charming stranger, who had handed me the copy of what had become one of my favourite books and exited into the night of the unknown. Where was he now? What were his thoughts on, well, anything? I felt I had to know!

In returning to the local pub, The Devonshire Arms, again and again with but one hope and a few pounds, I found that the disappointment dug deeper into my heart with each unsuccessful venture.

Was it this moment in isolation that brought me so low or was it instead all that had gone before? Was the stranger's absence that which stirred fresh demons of existential loathing from their slumbers or was it perhaps it ALL?

I drove myself quite mad wondering about his whereabouts, but sadly never saw him again; the only spark of hope I could see died before it could enlighten. The trapped inner scream began and I sensed it, but could not locate its source.

The spiritual children with their unending appetites for money and fame paid no heed to my limited triumphs or numerous woes, meanwhile I could not help but notice their every move: in scrolling through the news I would be inundated with information about the latest record, book or activities of the rich and famous coupled with detailed expositions of every fashion choice and physical feature of these stars.

From the hipsters to the politicians and the

vacuous celebrities it was obvious everyone was faking it, but few seemed to be really making it. I got the distinct sense that I was watching the disintegration of humanity in real time.

In my distress I decided to pay another visit to my medium, who told me that there was nothing wrong with me. Then why was I in so much pain, I reflected? Finally I had struck upon something I couldn't believe in and the cynic in me decided the whole thing was fraudulent and to be paid no mind: after all no one can be trusted, least of all oneself.

I had come to believe that about 80% of people weren't worth knowing, but the ones who were would get you through: wisdom scared most people, while knowledge escaped them.

"Why are people so horrible?" I would endlessly enquire from a beleaguered Johnny. "I'm not talking about you, or me, but the entire human species. Why can't we ever seem to make wise choices, but instead murder wisdom wherever it's found? What's wrong with us? Are we to be forever careering from catastrophe to disaster?"

However, Johnny had no real answers to placate me this time; a familiar hatred of life burrowed into my weary soul while happiness remained my biggest fear.

I wanted desperately to save the world, but in reality I could barely save myself: suicidal thoughts whirled as a storm in my mind, lightning bolts of despair and the thunder of past traumas distressed the environment of my very soul.

It was a wonder I was old enough to carry such

pain: most people my age were supposedly living their best lives with healthy bodies and ample years ahead of them. However, without good mental health I soon found life to mean preciously little.

I could only imagine that God didn't intend for me to live a calm life, and tried to weather my inner and outer storms with creativity, bravery and even occasional flair. For to rid myself of sorrow I tried many techniques, attempting to trick my mind into continuing this farce.

Mainly I felt as though the universe must, for some reason, want me to be here. And as long as that desire remained, so would I. Despite this, during my most melancholic moments, I had firmly decided that it was better to kill oneself than to kill anyone else.

After a few weeks of being unable to write due to my overwhelming depression, I picked up a pen and ventured again into the frontier of literature.

The Winter Of Our Understanding

We are slaves to our natures,
Chained to fates we do not understand,
And neglectful of our true power;
Our hopes have wilted as summer flowers
Before the lethal black ice appeared in this,
The winter of our understanding.

Chapter Thirty

"The shifting tides of the world can swallow or reveal at whim," I spoke, rather pretentiously, as Johnny and I discussed the possibility of Atlantis. It was a fairly coherent sentence for me at that point in time as sense seemed frequently elusive.

"We're all in a system which is fucking up the planet, none of us can escape," Johnny concluded after another day of frantic peace talks featuring multiple theories about how to rescue the human race from itself. "The trouble is we need about 17 revolutions," I wryly observed.

I had suddenly taken a liking to fashion design and made a t-shirt to wear to the pub saying "know yourself, be yourself, love yourself". I had expected people to care, but no one did.

To console myself from this latest episode of poor form on the part of humanity I returned to talk once again with Johnny.

"I feel like a flower growing in concrete," I confessed before a quote came to mind:
'Long live the rose that grew from concrete
When no one else ever cared!'
Tupac Shakur understood.

I played John Barry's Dances With Wolves soundtrack on my phone to ease the pain, the tinny goodness soothing my frazzled soul. Johnny also listened keenly – he appreciated the gentle cadences fully once he had turned the volume of his beloved BBC Radio 6 down.

"Have I told you my favourite line from this

film?" I enquired.

"Probably, but tell me again?" Johnny responded with a smile.

"There's no trail in life like the trail of a true human being." I let the words resonate.

"What do you think? Are we true human beings, Johnny? Is our journey a good one?"

"I hope so," he said warmly and the days continued to pass in this familiar pattern. We liked to believe that we were learning and growing with each kiss of the sun or envelopment of darkness, consciously evolving with every passing hour.

The first lesson of life, I had decided in the midst of the process, was to follow your intuition. After contemplating it intensely the night before I had come to believe that intuitions led to palaces beyond the capabilities of the imagination and riches beyond measure.

"You know, if I'd followed my heart I could have been a legend by now," I found myself saying out loud the next day. "Or else I could be dead..." My thoughts trailed off in the usual morbid directions.

"Death? Fuck death!" Johnny said with a grin.

He was looking extra-thin these days, though he had stuffed himself with his beloved garlic cloves in melted butter. No matter how much he ate and how frequently, his appetite for drugs was stronger still.

"What are you, a necrophiliac?" I joked facetiously.

"I said 'fuck death' not 'fuck dead bodies', you

sicko!" Johnny responded sharply. To clarify his point he then elaborated vividly, gesticulating wildly: "Fuck crawling along on your belly to please people until you get your state pension. Fuck paedo priests going to Heaven and gays going to Hell. Fuck waiting every second of your life thinking whether or not this day will be your last. Start to glimpse through and open the doors life shows you instead of making a fortress of your heart," Johnny spoke his vitriol as if he was on his death bed, imparting his final rather blue linguistic offerings to a beloved.

They were not his final words, though they were as it turns out some of the latter words of the evening: I went to bed troubled, wondering if Johnny was secretly speaking directly to me when he offered his advice to humanity.

"I love myself and I want to live" was repeated in my head the next day as a mantra after I had optimistically reversed the Kurt Cobain song title. I Hate Myself And I Want To Die was such a cop out: I felt that any mug could feel this way past the age of about twelve, but that the opposite message was seldom shared.

I'd have loved to say that I wasn't alone, but I so often was these days: alone in my thoughts, alone in my world and even alone in my soul; I spent my days waiting for a change which never came.

The afterlife increasingly appeared more important than life itself: I had an almost Egyptian awareness of the temporary nature of all living things and therefore always had one eye on what was coming next in an eschatological sense. It was quite an organised spectrum of existence which I had assembled in my psyche: learn from the past, enjoy the present and plan for the future.

Of course, all of my thinking about the afterlife brought me to the question of morality. I didn't consider drug use to be immoral or God wouldn't have invented drugs; it was humans who discredited and shamed those who even temporarily engaged with mind-altering substances.

I also didn't think sex outside of marriage was immoral if it was mutually consensual and joyous. In short, I did nothing wrong in my eyes.

For me the real evils were avarice, racism, misogyny, paedophilia, murder, rape, homophobia, classism, lies. In other words many of the behaviours the church had endorsed, permitted or turned a blind eye to. The real church in my way of seeing things, a place of deep worship and connection to God, lay deep within our own hearts; an inner altar we could all pray at night and day.

As a result, I often found myself talking to God throughout my life expressing gratitude for a meal, asking for a family member be surrounded with protective energy or praying for forgiveness for past mistakes: life was so much better when lived in a state of constant prayer.

Though it didn't feel that way I was supposedly in the prime of my life and it could be said that I was in a reasonable spiritual and emotional state in that I only thought about killing myself every few days, a vast improvement on earlier years. Several hours would pass when I wouldn't even dream of suicide; occasionally I even enjoyed my pitiful excuse for a life. Yet the swings and rollercoasters of contemplations left me, mentally speaking, sick and dizzy.

In terms of human archetypes there were two extremes in my perspective: one had their eyes fully open and saw virtually everything whilst the other was blind and saw nothing at all. I felt myself to be the former, but in seeing so much I had in time mutated, my third eye bloodshot and worn out as someone who had stared for too long at the Sun.

My writing began to reflect this bleakness of spirit, though my ability to create at all given the circumstances seemed miraculous.

All is love
In Heaven above,
Though below
It seems not so:
Friends betray,
Lovers stray
And flowers cease to grow.

"I think good, healthy, positive thoughts," I repeated in my head on a loop after a barrage of the opposite. I wasn't certain whether or not I was deluding myself, but my contemplations would have flooded my mind with rancid intellectual sewage had I not invented a psychological dam of some variety. Besides, words were all I could find at the best of times and had proved themselves most diverse.

Of course calm books and gentle films would have helped as well as such hotchpotch mantras, but there were not many of those about. It was all I could do to dredge up enough courage to face another day.

Was I to remain fundamentally alone in the battle to survive? Yes, friends and lovers came and went, but I found myself to be the only constant. I wondered at the strength of my own perceptions for though my greatest enemy was myself, I knew it not.

I recognised a gap in my knowledge and continued to probe and silently wonder.

"Perhaps human beings were all destined in their own ways to be bereft of allies in this most hopeless of wars, together as one in their isolated states? It could be the case that others were simply questionably real non-player characters - how was anyone to truly know?"

I had once again gone too far in my thinking for safety and needed to turn back from this intellectual pathway before I found myself completely internally lost.

Socialising for a while seemed sensible, though when I was arrogantly confronted by a fellow barfly who claimed to be "approaching enlightenment" I baulked at the suggestion.

"We're ALL approaching enlightenment! That's the whole deal. It's just some of us are more clumsy in our efforts," I protested, confident in the soundness of my reasoning.

"You're not even close, woman!" The stranger roared with laughter at his own joke before downing his pint and leaving abruptly. Clearly the bubble of his egotistical and even rather misogynistic worldview had been fatally pierced.

Thoughts which were destined never to be communicated gathered internally to the profound distress of my soul. I fought against the dying of the light: the youth which was sliding into the past, the relationships I could not hold together, the tears I refused to shed. Nevertheless it was quite a different environment to the one I had been brought up to expect and I battled the urge to sever my connection to this troubled region of the universe. I waged war with existence itself, but it was no use: I was growing older alone without financial security or my faculties wholly intact.

I wanted a house, a husband, a baby, acceptance. Yet what I found was emotional isolation followed by self-destructive tendencies and an unwanted sense of nihilism. Some people may well have thought that life meant nothing, but not me: in a healthy frame of mind I believed that every single thing meant everything. Even the way I wore my hair was in a sense connected to every other choice which had ever been made.

Though it was popular to think of life as meaningless, I often suggested that it was beneficial for those around me to see small yet very real significance in all there was. For whether the meaning within each thought, word and deed was visible or hiding, it was surely there awaiting discovery by someone who cared enough to really consider it.

As with the deciphering of hieroglyphs, I could sense there was symbolism hidden within life's events and moments. I just did not understand the source behind the labyrinth of synchronicities and illegitimate emotions.

Yet the human journey had only just begun in real terms. If the universe was 13.7 billion years old, as scientists decreed and homo sapiens emerged between 200,000 and 300,000 years ago then we could scarcely as a species boast of maturity and wisdom: human beings had only existed for the tiniest fraction of the universe's history, whether the product of chance or design, and often had trouble correctly identifying themselves let alone a creator.

What really bothered me was how little difference I could make to the bigger picture; whether I was sane or insane, clever or dumb, a hippy wild child or a fascist of the norm my actions seemingly fell like a stone into a deep well with water so shallow there was barely a returned sound.

The small effects I did have on life were worthy of note, though. When I returned home and made a simple dinner my mother felt reassured of the calibre of her parenting and when I picked my cousins up from school on the rare occasions I visited my more distant family their parents could breathe a sigh of relief at having a short moment to themselves.

Of course, I was in many ways the last person anyone would want around their children: my inner and outer worlds were whirlwinds of confusion, emotional negligence and distress in general. But still, I was vaguely functional and helped out where I could in small moments of mutual appreciation.

When alone with my tortures, however, I found I was losing the great war for my soul: I hated my life, or perhaps the state of being alive, along with the way in which my only sources of joy were considered either illegal or immoral. The dizzying ups and downs coupled with the unbearable constants proved the perfect conditions for total despair.

I needed to get away and the universe duly provided a temporary break in proceedings, the cage of her day-to-day existence shattering as I so wished.

Jessica, my long-term supposed friend at the time, was in a similar emotional boat to me, prone as she was to long bouts of anti-social despair and passive suicidal ideation. The slightly older young woman of thirty had three diagnosed mental health conditions and HIV among a host of other ailments. But, most importantly, she was fun. So when she suggested I accompany her to a friend's flat in London my naïve self didn't feel the need to think twice.

I had even introduced Jess to Taylor a few months previously, which had resulted in the Londoner proclaiming that Jess was the type of woman that he could fall in love with. When it came to substances, I perceived Jessica to be desiring love most of all, but declined to tell her of Taylor's affection knowing that Jess was ultimately in no state to nurture such a dalliance.

Jessica and I caught the train to London one rainy weekend and ended up in a friend's flat in some random region of the capital, eventually nipping to a corner shop to fetch snacks and supplies in increasingly dishevelled states.

The one thing that I concluded after a couple of days of wayward behaviour was how sweet, kind and intelligent Jessica's acquaintances were. Whether spiritual or atheist, straight or gay, ravers or rockers there was a gentility to this collection of characters which spoke of difficult childhoods and troubled futures: these youngsters had obviously known much pain in their short lives and therefore worked hard in order not to reproduce their more traumatic experiences.

They were good souls before they got swept up in the world, chained by concepts of materialistic achievement and torn apart by the jaws of meaningless competition. No more the child's eyes of innocence: those had been replaced by the steely stares of judgement.

Were you a pretty thing ripe for a group photograph, a sexual encounter or perhaps a romance of some duration? Did you possess the finances to purchase as well as consume the drugs you wished to sample? Could you have the attributes to glue the broken pieces of a heart back

together or would you prove yourself to be yet
another wild beast, all teeth and claws, in a
dangerous world? All these questions and more
were posed to me, a stranger to the strange, in the
briefest of glances.

As the intoxication peaked so too did the sense
of sheer euphoria; conversations marked by the
quick wit and erudite insights of the participants
were taking place wherever I looked, but Jessica
was busying herself by making a scene as soon as
we arrived. Drugged beyond sense and nightmarish
in her ranting, only after several hours of coercion
was she calm enough not to make herself a focal
point of distress and harsh words, having tried the
patience of even the most temporary of guests.

I tried to keep my head low, feeling myself to be
an alien in such a hedonistic environment: I did not
want to draw attention to my discomfort, my
relative innocence. I had only taken Tina a few
times and was unprepared for the more seasoned
nature of much of the debauchery: some of the
paraphernalia shocked and delighted in equal
measure as the scene evolved (or perhaps regressed
depending on your perspective).

Eventually Jess and I departed and once again I
returned to my family home in Cambridge to face
the wrath of my mother, the matriarch's fury
masking her deep-seated disappointment in her
offspring. I was in no mood for confrontation, but it
was happening whether I liked it or not.

I foolishly believed the best form of defence was
to attack and so embarked upon a ferocious verbal

assault only to find my intellectual blows all failed to land. Quite to the contrary, they awoke the beast in my mother. Towards the end of the confrontation I had to seriously question whether I was the great military leader of conversational warfare that I had always pictured myself as.

"Get a decent job, find a stable relationship, get your own place... You're just a stuck record, Mum!"

Louise was incensed at her offspring's words, her behaviour and even her very presence.

"No, YOU'RE the stuck record, Clara, and if you can't see that you must be blind or stupid - or both. I'll have you know that I am neither, though you may think of me as such. The parties, the boys, the loser friends... Can't you see that yours is not a life to be proud of? I must have raised a complete fool," Louise trailed off while on the brink of tears.

To appease the parental gods I joined the gym and got a short-lived new job in a shop. I wanted to extricate myself from the web of bad influences, but couldn't figure out how - there was seemingly nothing to replace it with. I didn't want to cut off all of my so-called friends in one fell swoop, but their collective way of life was causing too much friction.

As though life was a game of chess, I debated my next move. Perhaps the answer to all of my problems was to stop speaking to my Mum instead, though this seemed overly harsh and cruel. After all, I owed the life I barely wanted to this woman. Perhaps therein lay the root of the problem; my emotional cup brimmed over with a bitterness I was fighting in my own way to contain.

My parent's judgements and condemnations ostensibly came from a good place, but I was not and seemingly could never be the perfect daughter. Thus my sense of self-loathing and disappointment in the very fabric of my being continued to grow.

Why was I so incapable of making the right choices? At what point had I taken a wrong turn? Was there a way back, a diversion to redemption as my grandmother had so hoped for me?

Following the nasty disagreement with my mother I decided to take a walk. During the process of my stroll to Mill Road my emotions got the better of me: a single tear escaped from the inner well at first, but soon there was a flood to accompany it. One, two, three, four... Who could keep track of such a thing? After several minutes I was a state and broke into a run in order to find Johnny.

The thing that distressed me the most was that no one witnessing the scene asked if I was okay or enquired about my distress. In fact, I got the distinct impression that were I to rush up to groups of strangers and try to share my story they would only dismiss me in order not to wake their own existential discomfort. It was pointless trying to stir the spiritual sleepers, every great teacher of wisdom had found, and I defected from such a task in the face of certain defeat.

Tears streaming and suffering tangible, I opened Johnny's door as though it were the gate to Heaven itself: a single soul who cared enough to listen when I was at my most vulnerable provided wealth unknown by too many.

"It'll be okay, Clara. Believe in yourself and you will live to see your dreams; you have to move towards a brighter tomorrow in order to reach it," Johnny's soothing words comforted my broken soul. But he could see from my desperate eyes that they had not been enough, so he ventured onwards.

Meanwhile I was unsure what dreams he was referring to: I didn't have any visions of my future worth sharing, barely wanted anything anymore – not even to be here.

"The trouble with you is that you're extremely sensitive, yet always focus on the negative aspects of life and death (of which indeed there are many). You never see the blessings time has brought you," Johnny continued until the interruption inevitably came.

"What blessings? I have nothing, Johnny. Not a penny to my name or a hope in hell of living anything but my worst nightmares," I was convinced of the truth to the words I spat with sincere venom.

"You have so much, Clara... I'm your biggest fan! I cherish every word of yours: I'm your cheerleader with a shrine to your very existence in my heart. Remember wisdom is better than silver and gold. You are richer than you know!"

With that I felt slightly better. Whether they were nice words to soothe a troubled mind or considered concepts which came from the depths of

Johnny's being made little difference to me: they worked.

I suddenly felt as though I could face another day, maybe 10 at a push. Unfortunately there were so many more on the horizon, approaching as enemy soldiers armed with strife and expectations.

"What am I going to do, Johnny?"

"Just be, Clara. Just be."

"How are you, anyway?" I braved after a long pause of being. Though clearly hoping for a distraction from my own emotional turbulence, the opposite result occurred.

"I saw Ben today," Johnny reported.

"How was he?"

"Sad like the rest of us," Johnny confirmed solemnly and silently wondered when the revolution would come, if the point of critical mass required for drastic social change would be reached soon, whether he would ever know the cultural developments he so longed to live to see.

Much of the injustice he saw was rooted in economics and Johnny cursed Adam Smith, the father of capitalism, for his erroneous assessments of human needs.

Smith believed that humans were naturally self-serving, but that as long as individuals sought to fulfil their own needs, the society would function as a whole.

The Scotsman was clearly mistaken, in Johnny's opinion, as the Englishman watched the rich get richer and the poor get poorer, clutching his pension as a life raft.

"Capitalism simply doesn't work!" Johnny would rage, his previously calm ocean now stirred beyond all recognition. He took another drag on his medicine, but even that couldn't dissuade him from his anger.

Perhaps, indeed, his choice of consumption was allowing him to source the well of frustration which lay within his very soul and consequently release it in order to avoid incubating any toxicity. Wrath was his self-declared weakness among the seven deadly sins - it continued to reveal itself. However, on this occasion his vitriol was not, perhaps, entirely misdirected.

"Capitalism is breeding greed, competition and division. We need to amend the way our economies are run so that the needs of all are equally catered for. Human beings are acting as parasites: destroying natural resources, killing prophets and worshipping only GDP."

It was, after all, no secret that the trickle-down economic model had morphed into a system that was flooding upwards. Most powerlessly sat in awe of the deadly combination of avarice and ignorance exhibited by those at the acme of the free-market capitalist hierarchy.

Tax havens and oil money propelled ethically wayward individuals up the ladder of material success, but consequently left the general populace bereft of spiritual leadership. With all the principled greats now shot, the sheep were without adequate shepherds and wandered aimlessly across the perilous valleys of disenchantment.

The opposite of love was widely regarded to be fear. Therefore, the very worst affliction was to be scared of love and, though I had not delved deeply enough into my soul, heart and psyche to discover such a thing, it was this which was the real root of my issues.

Every time I got close to someone or something truly remarkable the same panic would set in: what if I was to lose it, the vase once full of life-giving water shattering before my very eyes? No, I couldn't bear even the thought! It was best to push my blessings away before they had the chance to mean anything to me, I had loudly subconsciously declared.

I decided to once again write my way through my deepest feelings as all true writers do.

Hell

Bombs drop;
People cry.
No one can decipher
For what cause they die.

The Emperor's a madman;
The politicians are all thieves.
Put your trust in nobody,
Least of all those who lead.

To imprint footprints on the path of progress
Is my lofty aim.
I find life oh so serious

While death is but a game.

Some win, others lose -
The lines are blurred
Between the darkness and the light
All at once the curtain could fall
Turning day into night.

I make my bed, I brush my teeth.
It's not enough to help those in need:
My sisters cry and my brothers wail
We're turning this world into a living Hell.

After scrawling my ideas onto a page I returned to my family home briefly while my mother was at work in order to wash some clothes and fetch some things. Meanwhile, unbeknownst to me, Johnny had been thinking - feeling even – during my absence and upon my return he had a speech prepared which moved my troubled soul.

"Clara please don't abandon your quest to eke every morsel of wisdom from this world and leave it a richer place in the process. I know those around you do the opposite: most people spit upon genuine wisdom and seem determined to leave this world a shell of its former self.

"But not you. You are a rare one, the watch on the beach which makes me believe in a higher power: if God can make someone as loving, passionate, thoughtful and truthful as you then He or She or It must be a force for good... Take these words because they are all that I have!" Johnny continued, emotion streaming from his every sinew.

"I can't give you the world or even make a single person truly listen to you and acknowledge the beauty of your soul. But I can show you the love you deserve, unconditional support and unwavering kindness. If that is still not enough to keep you here check the fridge!"

Though blown away by the power of my true friend's words I got up curiously and opened the fridge door, nearly losing my balance in the process as I tripped over discarded art and empty cans of booze.

Johnny had only gone and cooked one of his exquisite vegan extravaganzas with whole cloves of baked garlic drenched in butter as a delicious accompaniment. It was a simple stew, but it had become my favourite meal and Johnny knew it would be so special in my tear-stained eyes. I was so taken aback by the combination of thoughtfulness and the heartfelt emotion in his speech.

Although most of the food Johnny cooked was vegan or close to being so, my attempts at a vegetarian diet were often an issue. It was hard enough to find a suitable sandwich in a supermarket let alone avoiding such restrictions being a matter of contention around the dinner table with friends and relatives.

Did one have to participate in the murder of millions of innocent creatures in order to be deemed acceptable to the masses? I was sure the first person to highlight the horrors of the Holocaust must have appeared a little weird and against-the-grain, but nevertheless it had to be done. In my ideal world all sentient beings would have an equal right to life and I was determined to move towards that dream even as others swam in the opposite direction.

That evening with Johnny as my only companion, I realised that I had been heard; at last someone had really heeded my behavioural red flags waving vigorously as someone in pain: Johnny really loved me and had found ways to externalise his care seemingly just in the nick of time. It was the kind of friendship which occurs only fleetingly within a lifetime and with each passing day it seemed to grow stronger.

"You need to speak to me, Clara: there's very little difference between living and dying if you can't say how you feel."

"But thinking gets you killed, we all know that," I retorted.

"Life is too short not to say how you feel. And besides, sweetheart, we are all in the palm of God's hand merely waiting for it to close," Johnny whispered with raised eyebrows and a sense of resigned frailty.

"I want an apology from God for what I've been through - I've died a hundred times."
I paused to ingest some more toxins and consider my position.

"But you're still here," Johnny reassured and, as we were eating our meals, I braved a burning question.

"Johnny, what did you mean when you were talking about the watch on the beach? I didn't get that part at all, sorry!"

Johnny thought it common knowledge and tried hard not to be visibly disappointed in my lack of erudition.

"The watchmaker analogy was a teleological argument put forward by William Paley, a Peterborough philosopher who essentially argued that if you were to come across a watch on a beach you would assume that it had a designer. As it is with the world. As it was when I found you," Johnny explained, leaving unspoken sentiments hanging in the air between them.

"It's an argument for the existence of God," he clarified.

"So, when you see me you see my creator?"

"Can't you see mine?" Johnny said with a smile. "But some people shine with it, as you do. No one is special like you are to me." Clara feared Johnny's love would not be enough to save her, so tried to explain her side of things.

"I've always wanted to die, Johnny, I don't know why. It started when I was seventeen with a particularly bad bout of anorexia. It wasn't anything to do with anyone else, just a feeling that I'd had enough. You get old souls and young souls, why not push the boat out and suggest the plausibility of tired souls?

"If I was a medicine man with due authority I would declare myself such. But seeing as the ancient ways are all but dead I will question the existence of my very soul and fail to enquire about its condition."

"Sadly that's the way of it, milady!"

"I think we're suffering collective trauma from the way in which we are told that life will be A, B and C when actually it has numerous permutations. A 9-to-5 job, 2.4 children, stable marriage, car, bank account in credit and holidays twice a year is just not an achievable - even desirable - way of living for many people. Yet here we are, instructed that this blueprint is the key to Heaven on Earth and shamed into obtaining as many of these accolades as humanly possible lest we deviate from the pack. We break our backs to achieve others' dreams while our own get dusty on some inner shelf, put there because we were prematurely told they were impossible.

"And I'm tired, Johnny. I'm tired of the deafening bullshit, the corruption, manipulation of consciousness and focus on the material world which renders people like me surplus to requirements. And don't we just know it! With every party political broadcast which mentions the poor by name there is only an overt sense of condemnation.

"I had a roommate once who asked why the poor don't simply save more. This tornado of ignorance will engulf the entire planet if we let it, our tribal pasts buried in the mud of history and the wisdom of our experience - our living in harmony with nature - lost forever. Our previous selves are rejected as savages who had not yet learned of pride. Yet, in place of primal people, what monsters now stand? We still don't take care of one another. We still haven't developed societies which have earned the adjective civilised. Maybe it's an eternal quest," I tempered off.

"Learn and grow, milady," Johnny concluded.

With that I went to sleep in my room, happy for the first time in ages. I snuggled into my duvet as a cat into a lap and consciously practised gratitude for all that I had: food in my belly, wine on my tongue, a place to rest my head and a friend who genuinely cared. Was there any need for more?

It was at this point, just as I was laying my head down to rest, that a haunting voice came to me: it belonged to the homeless woman I had met several weeks ago now, begging me to be the reason someone believed in a higher power. How marvellous, I thought, that with Johnny's words the woman's wishes had somehow been fulfilled. I wondered with delirium at the meaning of it all and resolved to tell Johnny in the morning – if I indeed remembered! It was a struggle to recall everything that mattered, but at least I wasn't considered a complete idiot – a doofus, maybe?

Chapter Thirty-One

I had become wholly unimpressed by the world, but that didn't mean I wasn't a part of it. Every sense of frustration and desperation contributed to a picture broader than any eye could perceive.

I suddenly felt I had struck upon something and began to write furiously until it was worded correctly in my eyes. I then read my considerations aloud to Johnny amidst plumes of smoke and good vibes.

"We are not here alone, surrounded by the horror of the existential storm. We have a compass to direct us in every moment: intuition. It cannot guarantee a route to eternal happiness alone, but when coupled with the winds of reason and sails of discernment it can take us far on a spiritual voyage.

"Though waves and rain crash down, I've not drowned in water nor tears. My vessel stays strong thanks to my maker from whom every moment comes with a bow. Suffering feels everlasting, tears stream as rivers to seas of deep despair, but my heart withstands all of this in the name of love."

"All IS love, anyway," Johnny added his response coupled with a sweet smile.

"Those who know know and those who don't know don't matter," Clara confirmed.

"I disagree. Those who don't know should be taught," Johnny argued, wisely.

As I felt my faith calling me to act I returned to church and wrote a song to honour my experiences there. Watching the devoted souls go about their

rituals and bravely explore agape through their
words and actions could not help but leave a mark.
My writing reflected how moved my spirit had
been to be in the presence of sincere worshippers.

Street Preacher

Stormy seas surround me -
Thank God I found you, Jesus!
'Cause we all need a friend on whom we can
depend.

I'm on my knees again tonight.
And if you need a hug or ear
Your goal's inside,
But we all need a friend on whom we can depend.

I'm talkin' Jesus,
I'm talkin' 'bout Jesus,
I'm screaming "Jesus"
Like a street preacher!

Seasons come and then they go,
Yet more and more and more we know.
We still need a friend on whom we can depend.

I fought valiantly in the battle against my mental
afflictions, yet still my demons plagued me.
    "How are you feeling?" Johnny enquired.
"I feel like I'm going to be fucked-up forever," I
replied bleakly.

"So, stable then!" Johnny nodded and I couldn't help but laugh at both him and life itself.

I thought to myself that if only rich people would start to stand up for the poor then humanity would be on a slippery slope towards equality, but there was no sign of that happening in the near future. Instead things trundled on with a downward arc to a trajectory that the 1% fought hard to maintain. Divide and rule was, after all, a very long game played by those at the top of the economic system and there was only ever going to be one winner: the rich themselves.

They had a lot to answer for, these dwellers of super yachts and climate criminals. Who would have thought that taking private jet flights for the distance of a short drive would prove so tolerable to so many? Still the grossly wealthy harped on in the environmental conferences and board rooms about the need for social change, all the while ignoring their own advice: personal responsibility had a price few were willing to pay and as a result hypocrisy spread and mutated as a plague.

I was not certain whether my writing was improving or deteriorating in the midst of my woes - as with all things it was seemingly a rollercoaster ride.

All I really knew was that I yearned for the day when a mother would no longer have to say to her daughter "there's still so much to do", a time when, for even just a single moment, total equality would be theirs to enjoy.

But for now my feelings were printed on my t-shirt which read "Too many predators, not enough justice!" I got an array of comments as a result of wearing it to the pub, everything from support to derision.

One man even went so far as to claim during their discussion that most accusations of sexual assault were false, but I did not consider it my place to completely refurnish a sparse mind. Knowing nothing about anything was obviously in fashion, caring less so. Still, I maintained my faith in my fashion statement and refused to kowtow to the need for absolutely unwavering external validation.

Far from the spiritual guru I had expected to become given my extensive existential excavations, I felt vulnerable, as though the slightest gust of astrological wind would blow me away; a moon out of alignment or a planet in retrograde could totally tip me over the edge. After another awful dating experience I was in full feminist flow at Johnny's.

"I don't understand why men are so horrible in general! All across the world they make up laws which they themselves declare to be gods' which prohibit women and girls from equality, education and independence.

"Men make war with each other en masse, raping and murdering innocent women in children in their path, all in the name of flags or gods. Their egos cause them to make deities in their own image, projecting their cruelty onto the divine: the whole thing is a vicious circle. We carry our pasts as a burden of bloodshed and horror, desperately offloading the weight we are crippled by onto our offspring who often do not thank us for the task of carrying on this charade.

"If you start seeing a man these days he'll most likely make it abundantly clear that he doesn't want a relationship. If you do miraculously make it to the stage of being formally entwined he's unlikely to disguise his desire for other women and may well cheat sooner or later.

"The most beautiful woman in the world couldn't dissuade many men from infidelity, so why bother with the rigour and upkeep of pursuing physical perfection? Woe betide the woman who attains such a feat only to realise she still has nothing of any real substance in her hands.

"How has this devolution of morality been allowed to happen? Nowadays good men kill themselves and bad men flourish while true gentlemen belong purely in museums!" I never gave up hope of finding a good man, though he was proving to be a needle in a deep and rancid haystack.

A love song to no one came to me and I wrote as if possessed, focusing on rhymes and images as though someone would one day care.

I Wish I Was With You

Pass that quart of vodka -
I have an appointment with a nasty hangover.
I know I've been drinking,
But I assure you I mean every word I slur.

The Watch On The Beach

I'm lying when I say
I'm happy on my own.
I truly, truly, truly wish I was with...

He asks me if I love him,
But he only gets me yawning on reply.
But you can tell I really like him,
Because every time I see him
I run a mile.

I say and do an awful lot of things
That I don't really mean,
But I truly, truly, truly wish I was with...

Skylines are so comforting
When you awake from a particularly bad dream
And soft words sound twice as kind
When spoken by a like mind.

But what used to make me happy
Now only makes me sad:
I wish I was with you.

So quote Hippocrates and Socrates
And all the clever things stupid people say.
What's philosophy, anyway?
Just a voluntary headache!

I say love can seem less of a blessing
And more a Devil in disguise.
And life feels like a bad birthday present

We must pretend we like.

But not when I'm with you,
Not when I'm with you.
I wish I was with you,
I wish I was with you.

After its completion I was again at a loose end.
Nothing made sense anymore: my life was a
constant snafu and I abased myself even in my own
mind.

Looking back, if I had learnt anything in life it
was to believe in myself. Yet presently I was
trapped in a nightmare, unsure whether I was even
asleep, awakening in states which made me wish I'd
never awoken at all.

There didn't seem to be any light breaking
through, but frankly one had to bring it. I wrote
scattered phrases, which moved through my
consciousness as driftwood upon a sea of
discontentment.

Prisms of understanding shine in my mind,
Light reflecting purely from the divine.

Realisation comes with cutting claws
As humans all are born with flaws.

Enlightenment does not come when you wait;
It comes when you learn to believe in your fate.

I trusted only in the divine, but in the past I had extended that trust to mere mortals. It was, in hindsight, a mistake I had paid for dearly. Now, when adrift and alone, I grappled with a future I could not bear to face. Not even Johnny was proving to be trustworthy: was suggesting acid for breakfast conducive to my happiness? There was only one way to find out.

As the circles formed and the colours played, I found myself deeply and profoundly disturbed. Terrorism was the theme of the day and I breathed in and out meditatively while watching the images swirl all about me. I was afraid and unsure whether mass consciousness was a state of mind I even wanted to tap into.

Nevertheless, the drug had taken hold and minutes passed which felt like hours. Eventually hours passed which felt like days and I emerged, bleary eyed and overly sensitive, from my previous state of mind. The cycle of death and rebirth had sped up to the point that the night had contained many deaths, yet the day had gifted many rebirths.

Johnny insisted afterwards that he'd had a wonderful time and proceeded to word it in a feeble sense, despite all of his expertise in elocution and vocabulary: words seemed small and weak compared to the might of the hallucinogenic experience.

Chapter Thirty-Two

In noticing my sense of stability once again slipping, Johnny sought compliments to offer me from deep within himself.

"You are a funny mix of traits I have yet to fully discern. In the headlights of life, you are wide-eyed as a deer and your calls for justice are a beacon for so many. Suffice to say that, as with a particularly intricate and heartfelt painting, you have elements it would take many years to fully comprehend. But so far I have experienced glimpses of a palatial heart."

With that, Johnny's serenading of my distraught soul came to an end. Yet while offering my heartfelt thanks for his words and sentiments, I was interrupted.

"I only hold a mirror to your brightly shining light, milady" he insisted, with a visceral passion which temporarily overwhelmed his audience of one.

I was slumped on the wine-stained couch in a manner which suggested I was absorbing my feelings as a thirsty plant in the sun's rays of real love.

While the spiritual children scrambled around for earthly riches and fleeting pleasures, I prided myself on consciously being on the road to enlightenment. The vastness of my inner world was accessed through prayer or, conversely, inebriation Yet it was seemingly always available. As a castle with a moat, it only needed a drawbridge to reach. It was in this sense that my soul merely awaited a choice: a simple decision to abandon what was temporary and embrace the eternal.

Safety lay within the walls of this spiritual fortress; protection from the howling winds of ignorance, idiocy and sorrow. The Goddess within me was raging, screaming and clawing for higher plains.

I found these elevated landscapes, once again, through words: inspired and intoxicated, I wrote as if the fate of my eternal soul depended upon the quality of my literary output.

Higher Plains

I want to go to the highest places,
Near to God.
Away from faces of judgement,
Faces of fear.

Each to their own,
But none too selfish.
Thinking of yesterday's
Such a waste of time
To higher minds.

Despite the perceived quality of my words these days I wasn't the woman I could have been and I knew it: a variety of opportunities had presented themselves to me upon life's pathway, few of which I'd taken with any real aplomb. Mostly I just coexisted with my fellow human beings when ideally I would have become some kind of leader by now.

Instead I found myself to be residing in the shadows of my past mistakes, rich only in the currencies of kindness and compassion. Unfortunately, the world did not reward such intangible qualities economically, socially or formally, and it seemed no wonder I had turned to God given the tornado of cruelty which had surrounded me from birth.

Was it a surprise I had consciously wished to die many times? Wasn't every moment simply the equation of what had gone before combined with one's own volition? The result - my existence - was displeasing to me: my soul had incarnated in order to love yet was encountering an excess of hatred. There was too much abandonment in this world and not enough devotion, I surmised.

Meanwhile I was devoted purely to truth, which was as unwelcome in this world as the prophets who preached it.

In this sense I was in certain moments noble, a queen without the need for a crown. At other times the weight of the world dragged me down into a netherworld frequented by terrifying demons.

However, at this point in time I had made my peace with death despite others still warring against it: the universe wanted me here for some unknown reason and, as a foot soldier in this great battle, I could only obey my biological order to survive.

I ventured onwards and, before taking a group photo on a night out, once again fixed my hair in the bathroom. I straddled the tectonic plates of vanity and insecurity as everyone did in their youths, violent spasms of judgment always threatening to erupt. Were my teeth straight and white enough? Was my make-up becoming? It would take me many more years to find my comfort zone, but for a moment I wondered at my reflection as its beauty overwhelmed my drunken senses.

As I stared with bleary eyes I hardly recognised my face as my own and momentarily began to cry inside at the thought of the wrinkles yet to come.

Yet in checking the collection of photographic spoils I felt only a sense of revulsion. Good photos proved hard tasks: the camera may have stolen from the moment something that could never be returned, but in doing so captured that which would otherwise be forgotten.

In returning from my booze-fuelled adventure I continued to dwell upon the deeper meaning of that which I was experiencing while nursing my hangover in Johnny's spare room.

I had heard the theory that humans designed their own lives before birth in order to evolve spiritually, forming pacts with soulmates in the spirit world whom they would at chosen times encounter upon their journeys. The Hindus referred to a personal pathway called dharma which was either correctly navigated or not and would potentially lead to moksha (escape from samsara or the cycle of reincarnation).

Yet if it was the case that all was planned prior to incarnation I felt the decisions had been poorly thought through, my supposed accomplices had let me down, my script almost too pointless to tolerate.

My profound disappointment was felt to an acute degree; now, in the midst of the process, I must live with the consequences of either my own failings or God's - I was even unsure who to blame for the sheer horror I was enduring. Seeing as God was perfection itself, could it be that the responsibility was secretly all my own?

Yes, on the surface life could have been worse. I generally had food in my belly and a safe place to rest. Indeed, people were dying to attain such physical comforts as I had grown accustomed to. But, being empathetic to an unhealthy degree, I found myself flinching at every bloody meat product on the supermarket shelves, baulking at the idea of spending my time betting on horses that may well die in the middle of their races and finding it galling to be told that I was ruled by those whose favourite pastime was murdering pheasants for sport.

It seemed to me that in order to maintain some semblance of inner peace one had to turn a blind eye to such injustices to a certain extent. If someone slaps another person without reason, the first in history to ever do such a thing, then - as Jesus advised - the recipient of this violence must find it within herself to be the first to forgive.

The alternative was escalation and humans had found that this route could be wandered down further than any sadist would find desirable, ultimately rendering all of humanity at least temporarily lost.

I was as usual trying to figure out what to do tomorrow. It was a Saturday and I had to work until 5pm, then go to my favourite pub The Pickerel with a friend, followed by a poetry reading at 6pm. That meant I had £24 until Monday and three social engagements.

I had also volunteered at St. Barnabas and been invited to lunch with the vicar. I had met him several times and always wanted to pour my heart out to him, but felt the need to kept things formal. A half-pint with Arabella, an orange juice and £5 entry fee for the poetry reading? It was no use, I would have to borrow money from my mother - again.

It was as Plato said: "The greatest wealth is to live content with little." Although he was no doubt a raging misogynist, I tended to agree with him on this point.

I spent the evening practising the poems with Johnny, who advised me to the best of his abilities.

Chapter Thirty-Three

In my suffering I had emerged as a nomad when it came to philosophical positions on the subject of suicide. Occasionally it seemed horrific: the logistics terrifying and the aftermath uncertain, a decision made only by those completely lost in a feral cyclone called the mind.

On other days it seemed impossible to ignore the option of ceasing your own pulse and escaping this living, breathing hell. I became unsure and ran for the hills should anyone try to breach the subject with me. Only the very few had played priests temporarily and been the recipients of my truest confessions.

Having said that, as the soft sun caressed my face and the cool breeze rustled my hair I knew that I was blossoming as a rose and found a sense of contentment in my physical flourishing.

I had spoken with focus and conviction at the poetry gathering the previous evening, yet despite the audience giving heartfelt applause there remained a gaping hole in the very core of my being. I continued to write poems of deep despair in order to satiate my need to create and in writing I felt something resembling optimistic clarity.

I decided in a moment of bursting optimism that I wouldn't want to be anyone else after years of yearning to be any man, woman or child except myself: my chaos was uniquely my own and I wouldn't have it any other way.

Free will was a double-edged sword; one had to appreciate its power and exercise it with real skill. So far in life I had wholly failed in this respect, but that didn't mean that I wasn't evolving all the time.

Yet after temporarily falling in love once again with life, the following day was more horrific than I could bear. It was a day that would punch you in the throat and kick you in the bollocks, even if you were unlucky enough to have been born without them.

Sensitive though I was, the origins of my negative emotions were relatively innocuous: in the wake of the #MeToo movement I read that recorded rapes had jumped from 1,068 per year in the UK in 1981 to 6,611 per year. Predictions were then made that this figure would increase tenfold in the coming years should nothing be done to stop the trajectory.

I couldn't bear to think about it, was triggered beyond my ability to cope: it raised memories of my own dark experiences with men which were rarely thought of let alone spoken about. Feeling as a piece of steak in a forest of wolves, I turned the music louder and pretended to have a good time.

But it was too late. The rollercoaster of my emotions had become too much to bear, the ups and downs were increasing in intensity, but also in their prevalence.

I once again overthought my individual position as well as the wider landscape I observed and in my self-analysis I found a distinct sense that I'd been emotionally robbed - I thought myself nothing more than an obedient little cog in a fucked up system. I would have glued myself to banks but for my cowardice: I found that I preferred to stay away from the law and explore the outer perimeters of alienation, but this was to eventually prove fatal to my wellbeing.

I felt that I was merely surviving instead of thriving and began to passionately resent even that state of affairs. Despite Johnny's best efforts and my collection of ramshackle associates, I felt alone, grieving an unstable past and living only within the palaces of a handful of scattered happy memories rather than in the destitution of the present moment. I was by now consciously lost and prayed to God that I would find the right path in time, though I felt the years slowly slipping away. It seemed faintly ridiculous to see any semblance of kindness in the future, anyway – after all, the passing of time will kill us all sooner or later.

I only wished the process was quicker as I began to reflect upon the decisions I'd made, finding to my profound despair that the great turning points of my life had been passed as though life was an obstacle course and every hurdle had been collided with as opposed to navigated. It was as though I was a dog with too short legs and could not help but to fell each plank.

I saw when I really looked within myself the stark reality of a troubled life where nothing but time had been overcome: it had come to the point where I could see no lessons learnt, no tears heeded by the divine. I hurtled towards an early death as a plummeting hippo seeking to be caught by a flimsy circus net. I then looked around for the nearest lethal weapon in Johnny's kitchen when he had temporarily left my side and, without care for the consequences or who would discover my bloody corpse, I did my very best to flee from the incessant horrors of this world.

Epilogue

I couldn't bring myself to write of Johnny finding me, bloody and alone, or his rapid decay from that point on: those were torture chambers best left unvisited. However, the shadowy recollections remain, lodged in my mind akin to the moment we met.

Since finishing my manuscript I have had a disjointed sense of peace: yes, I have communicated my deepest feelings, but do I like myself? It will take me years to adjust my most troubling behaviours, eliminate false allegiances and build a fortress around myself which only the very pure of heart can penetrate. In following such methods I find that a mild yet euphoric sense of contentment can be evoked.

I have established through the heady cocktail of time and experience that good hearts are rare, but I am also certain that they exist. They may stand out as watches on beaches - sometimes broken beyond repair with cogs and hands strewn across the shore – but their very presence provokes the mind to examine ever more thoroughly the wonders of existence.

Johnny, my dear friend who dwarfed all hyperbolic praise through the calibre of his numerous good qualities, had taken badly my decision to end my life. He refused to visit me in the hospital or answer my calls when I rang during my recovery. In short, he never forgave me.

The next thing I knew he was gone.

My trajectory prior to my suicide attempt alarmed him, of course, but the shock of him dying before me was sobering. I also hadn't expected his passing to dovetail so profoundly with my own decision to live.

After his departure from this world I was reunited with his diaries and, amidst more floods of entirely justified tears, recalled through his elegant daily entries the moment I had put my head on his shoulder and told him I loved him, the way he had given me candid drawings of myself every Christmas, the poems I had thrown away that he had kept without my knowledge.

It wasn't Johnny's fault that I lost control of my life temporarily: he was my guiding star, a shining light in the pitch black night of my hopelessness.

I thought of him often after he left us and even went to his memorial in the midst of my writing process; a cacophony of his words ringing in my very soul, I was determined to capture the otherworldly beauty of his undying spirit.

I think deep down Johnny wanted to prove life was forever a party. Unusually for him, he was very wrong, but that didn't mean life was not worth living: as metal honed by the white heat of suffering, we are designed with an intricacy acknowledged only by those who love.

It was Johnny who showed me the fluidity of friendship, the highs and the lows intertwining as waves in the stormy seas of human emotion.
It was I who had abandoned ship and left him to feel his love was worthless.

How could I repair such damage if not by making a life worth living in his absence? Indeed, Johnny's passing has proved to be the foundation on which I shall build my future life. The extinguishing of his flame has already fundamentally altered my very anatomy: all-nighters have become a thing of the past along with acid trips and promiscuity.

I may never be able to travel back in time in order to correct my plentiful mistakes. But I shall endeavour to venture onwards, depleted of my most cherished company and the audacity of youth.

In my excessive pride I know all the while my humble literary offering shall remain as a snapshot of my misspent youth, a dissection of my troubled mind, a depiction of a seemingly permanently broken heart. It will at the very least shock and appal the righteous and well-raised, stir those with the capacity for compassion and, ultimately, eulogise a friendship which now lives only in memories.

Printed in Great Britain
by Amazon